PENGUIN BOOKS

The Oracle of Change

Alfred Douglas has been interested in magic, mysticism, symbolism and the occult from an early age. He has made a special study of the esoteric traditions of East and West as revealed in such works as the I Ching and the ancient pack of Tarot cards.

After a childhood spent in seclusion among the Pennine hills and moors of Yorkshire, he gained admission to an arcane order which had been long-established in the British Isles, and led the life of a student for some years. It was during this period that he began preparing *The Oracle of Change*. Alfred Douglas has been instrumental in founding an arcane school which he now directs in London, and is at present writing a book on the meaning and use of the Tarot.

ALFRED DOUGLAS

The Oracle of Change

HOW TO CONSULT THE I CHING

Illustrated by David Sheridan

PENGUIN BOOKS

Penguin Books Ltd, Harmondsworth, Middlesex, England
Penguin Books Australia Ltd, Ringwood, Victoria, Australia

—

First published by Victor Gollancz, 1971
Published in Penguin Books 1972

—

Copyright © Alfred Douglas, 1971
Illustrations copyright © David Sheridan, 1971

—

Made and printed in Great Britain
by Richard Clay (The Chaucer Press) Ltd,
Bungay, Suffolk
Set in Linotype Plantin

To Jo Sheridan

Contents

Part One: Introductory

Part Two: The Text of the I Ching

7

Appendices

Illustrations

Part One: Introductory

CHAPTER I

The Oracle of Change

THE I Ching (pronounced Yee Jing), or Oracle of Change, is one of the oldest books in the world. Although its origin is lost among the myths of prehistoric China, the elements of its profound wisdom were undoubtedly formulated more than 4,000 years ago.

Its purpose is to reflect the changes that are constantly operating throughout all levels of the universe; the cycles and tides of fortune which we must learn to know and ride if we are to achieve success.

This ancient Chinese oracle enables us to glimpse something of these mysterious rhythms, and to realign our lives so that we are living more in harmony with the laws of nature.

Unlike many other methods of divination, you will find that the I Ching does not simply foretell future events and then leave you to cope with them as best you may. It offers sound advice on how to act in such a way that the future can be faced and experienced in the best possible manner.

By giving you an insight into the forces that guide your fate it enables you to plan ahead with assurance, aware of the processes being worked out through your life, and in a position to turn them to your advantage.

If the answer you receive from the oracle is auspicious you can push ahead with your plans confidently; if caution is advised you can prepare for hidden snags; if the indications are evil you can alter your plans accordingly and prepare for difficulties ahead.

The I Ching also has a second function. Designed to throw light on the hidden world behind appearances, it acts as a guide to the mysteries of your own unconscious self. Conscious actions and attitudes are to a great extent the result of unconscious motivations, and the oracle, when consulted by someone who is in sympathy with it, can give intuitive insight into the working of the inner self.

Unlike more limited methods of divination it does not simply tell you what is going to happen, but instead reveals why things are as they are and suggests what you can do about it. The final decision is yours; you remain the master of your ultimate fate.

*

The philosophies of both major Chinese religions, Taoism and Confucianism, are to be found within the I Ching's pages. Lao-tse, the founder of Taoism and a near contemporary of Confucius, based much of his teachings on the wisdom of the oracle, and Confucius himself may have written the first of a series of commentaries on it. These commentaries (all of which are traditionally ascribed to Confucius) still survive to form about half the text of modern editions.

According to the Analects (VII, xvi) Confucius once said: *If some years were added to my life, I would devote fifty of them to the study of the oracle, and might then avoid committing great errors.*

He made this statement when he was well into his seventies, and we are told that during the final years of his life he devoted so much time to the study and interpretation of the oracle that the leather thongs binding his copy wore out and had to be replaced three times.

The I Ching has retained its eminent reputation through subsequent centuries. In every age its guidance has been sought by Chinese philosophers, statesmen, warriors, and ordinary people when faced with an important decision or major undertaking.

The tradition is still maintained today in many communities, although officially the oracle has fallen into disuse on the mainland of China. It is widely studied in the modern universities of Japan, and is employed in business negotiations in many parts of South-east Asia.

The Oracle of Change was virtually unknown in the West until 1882, when the first significant English translation by James Legge was published. Legge disapproved of the book's function as an oracle; he did not explain how it could be used to foretell the future, and his painstaking, scholarly translation never became widely known except as an Oriental curio.

16

Nevertheless, Western interest in the I Ching has been growing steadily in recent years, stimulated largely by the findings of the great psychologist Dr C. G. Jung.

Jung discovered that the oracle's answers to his questions were always meaningful and often showed a deep insight into the problem at hand. This insight was sometimes so startling, Jung claimed, that he almost found himself believing the legend that a living being of great wisdom resides within the pages of the book.

In his autobiography *Memories, Dreams, Reflections*,* Jung has described his first journey into the world of the I Ching: 'I would sit for hours beneath the hundred-year-old pear tree, the I Ching beside me, practising the technique by referring the resultant oracles to one another in an interplay of questions and answers. All sorts of undeniably remarkable results emerged – meaningful connections with my own thought processes which I could not explain to myself.'

Jung recorded his thoughts on the I Ching in a brilliant introduction to Richard Wilhelm's German translation of the work which was first published in 1929. An English edition appeared in 1949, under the title *The I Ching or Book of Changes*, and the oracle found a new and enthusiastic readership.

This present version of the Oracle of Change comprises the original texts of King Wên and the later interpretations of his son Tan, the Duke of Chou, passages which form the heart of the work and which are known to have been composed over 3,000 years ago, with the addition of selected commentaries.

Here is all that is needed to consult the oracle and gain reliable advice, clear guidance, and insight into any question.

*Recorded and edited by Aniela Jaffé, translated from the German by Richard and Clara Winston. Published in London by Collins and Routledge & Kegan Paul, 1936. New York: Pantheon Books, 1961.

CHAPTER 2

The History of the I Ching

DURING the Lungshan period of Chinese prehistory, which flourished 4,000 years ago, a simple method of foretelling the future was used which involved the burning of a cow's shoulder-blade while a question was being asked. The heat produced cracks in the bone and a skilled interpreter then deduced the answer to the question by the position and shape of the cracks.

As time went by this method became more elaborate and ritualized. The question was first carefully inscribed on the shoulder-blade, into which a circular depression had previously been made. The tip of a heated bronze rod was then applied to the depression, and the cracks that resulted on either side of the bone were analysed.

Another favourite method consisted of burning a tortoise-shell and interpreting the cracks created in it by the heat.

The tortoise, symbol of stability and longevity, was held in great veneration; its shell was one of the sacred things ordained by Heaven to be favourable for oracular use.

There is a suggestion here of the origin of the I Ching. According to a very old tradition, the eight basic trigrams of the oracle were discovered on the back of a sacred tortoise.

The finding of these eight symbols is attributed to Fu Hsi, the mythical First Emperor of China who is reputed to have lived over 4,500 years ago.

One of the ancient commentaries on the I Ching described the discovery thus: *In ancient times, when Pao Hsi (i.e. Fu Hsi) ruled all things under heaven, he looked up and contemplated the bright patterns of the sky, then looked down and considered the shapes of the earth.*

He noted the decorative markings on birds and beasts, and the appropriate qualities of their territories.

Close at hand he studied his own body, and also observed distant things.

From all this he devised the eight trigrams, in order to unveil the Heavenly processes in nature and to understand the character of everything.

Although this legend may not be true in the literal sense, it does reflect the kind of inspiration which went into the creation of the Oracle of Change.

The broken and unbroken lines of the oracle were devised to represent the fundamental principles of existence. The unbroken line ——— is called Heaven, or Yang, and signifies the positive, masculine, active pole of nature. The broken line —— —— is called Earth, or Yin, signifying the negative, feminine, passive pole.

To show the interaction between these two opposites the two lines were combined in pairs to form the greater and lesser Yang and the greater and lesser Yin:

══	Greater Yang	═ ═	Greater Yin
─ ═	Lesser Yang	═ ─	Lesser Yin

A further line was then added, making eight possible three-lined figures, or trigrams:

To each of the trigrams was given a name and certain basic attributes:

☰	Ch'ien	Heaven	Active	Father
☱	Tui	Lake	Joyful	Youngest Daughter
☲	Li	Fire	Clinging	Second Daughter
☳	Chên	Thunder	Arousing	Eldest Son
☴	Sun	Wind	Gentle	Eldest Daughter

☵ K'an	Water	Dangerous	Second Son
☶ Kên	Mountain	Immovable	Youngest Son
☷ K'un	Earth	Responsive	Mother

The trigram Ch'ien represents the masculine principle of Heaven, or pure Yang, being made up of three solid lines; the trigram K'un represents the feminine principle of Earth, or pure Yin, and is made up of three broken lines.

The other six trigrams are comprised of the possible combinations of these two opposing, but complementary, aspects of Tao, the basic stuff of the universe. Appropriately, they are thought of as a family – father, mother, and six children.

The eight trigrams were used in an early form of divination, and are often depicted in Chinese art as rotating in a never-ending circle around the interlocking symbols of Yin and Yang:

The dark area (Yin) of the inner circle contains a white dot and the light area (Yang) contains a black dot; this teaches that even in their purest state each pole contains the seed of the other. Change operates even at the level of primal polarity.

The next important stage in the development of the I Ching took place around the year 1150 B.C., towards the end of the Shang dynasty. The last Shang Emperor, Chou Hsin, was an incompetent ruler under whose jurisdiction much of the empire was reduced to chaos and disorder.

During these difficult times the province of Chou in Western China was governed by a feudal lord called Wên, an able administrator who enjoyed great popularity.

To have such a reputation in those times was a decided liability, and in 1143 B.C. the Emperor ordered Wên's arrest. He was imprisoned in Yin, the Imperial capital which was located near the present-day city of Anyang in Honan province.

Here, while under constant threat of death, Wên studied the eight mystic trigrams.

By combining the eight trigrams in pairs he arrived at sixty-four six-lined figures, or hexagrams. He then went on to name each one and add an explanatory text. Each part of the text was derived from the significance of two trigrams combined.

For example, hexagram No. 11, entitled *Peace*:

is made up of trigram K'un, *The Responsive*:

over trigram Ch'ien, *The Active*:

Hexagram No. 53, *Gradual Advance*:

is a combination of trigram Sun, *The Gentle*:

over trigram Kên, *The Immovable*:

A year after his imprisonment friends working on Wên's behalf secured his release.

Not long after this the forces of Chou rebelled against the Emperor. In 1027 B.C. the capital was captured and the Emperor killed; the Shang dynasty was ended.

Unfortunately the struggle was not yet over; after a short period of peace rival factions began fighting for the right to the throne, and peace was only really achieved after the city of Yin had been totally destroyed.

The final victory was won by Wên's son Tan, the Duke of Chou, who became the true founder of the Chou dynasty.

Forty years after the hexagrams had first been devised, the Duke of Chou expanded his father's work on them. After studying Wên's text on the hexagrams he added his own interpretation to each single line; a total of three hundred and eighty-four separate passages.

It was at this time that Wên was awarded the posthumous title of 'King Wên', by which he has been known ever since.

The complete work, consisting of King Wên's sixty-four hexagrams and accompanying text, plus the Duke of Chou's interpretations of the lines, became widely known throughout the Chou empire under the title Chou I (The Change of Chou).

In the early part of the fifth century B.C. Confucius studied the Chou I, and may have written one of the commentaries on it which are attributed to him. Other commentaries composed by pupils and later followers of the Sage were added, until they formed a volume almost as large as the original work of King Wên and his son.

The oracle became officially recognized as one of the five Confucian Classics, and was named the *I Ching*, or Classic of Change.

The Confucian I Ching was deeply respected and its philosophy exerted a profound influence over many aspects of Chinese life. The great teacher Lao-tse (who might have been a contemporary of Confucius) must have seen in the I Ching a teaching close to his own philosophy; important decisions of all kinds were based on its advice, and men tried to live their lives in accordance with its precepts.

In the year 213 B.C. a great tragedy occurred. The Emperor at that time was Ch'in Shih Huang Ti, famous as the builder of the Great Wall of China. He was the first Emperor to unite large areas of China under a single rulership, and saw himself as the founder of a new epoch.

He readily agreed when he was advised by his minister Li Ssu to order the burning of all ancient literature; only those classics dealing with divination, medicine, and farming were to be spared as being essential to the successful ruling of the Empire.

The edict was carried out with great thoroughness. Over four hundred and fifty scholars were executed on charges of concealing forbidden books, and many more were condemned to forced labour on the building of the great wall.

Only the high reputation of the I Ching as a classic of divination led to its survival at this time.

During the Ch'in and Han dynasties (third century B.C. to third century A.D.) powerful schools of magicians arose who practised an occult form of Taoism and concerned themselves with the search for the Elixir of Immortality.

They adopted the I Ching and reinterpreted it in the light of their own esoteric doctrines; but in the latter half of the third century A.D. the young and brilliant scholar Wang Pi reaffirmed the essentially mystical side of the original work and emphasized its value as a philosophy of life.

This is substantially the version of the oracle that has come down to us today, in the form of modern Chinese editions, and in Western translations.

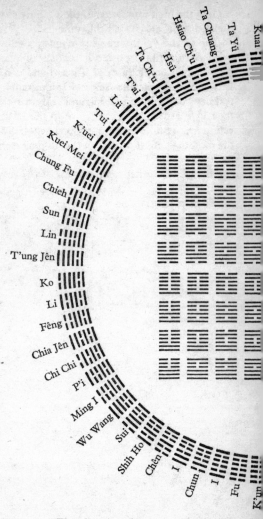

The sixty-four hexagrams displayed in the

Kuai
Ta Yü
Ta Chuang
Hsiao Ch'u
Hsü
Ta Ch'u
T'ai
Lü
Tui
K'uei
Kuei Mei
Chung Fu
Chieh
Sun
Lin
T'ung Jên
Ko
Li
Fêng
Chia Jên
Chi Chi
P'i
Ming I
Wu Wang
Sui
Shih Ho
Chên
I
Chun
I
Fu

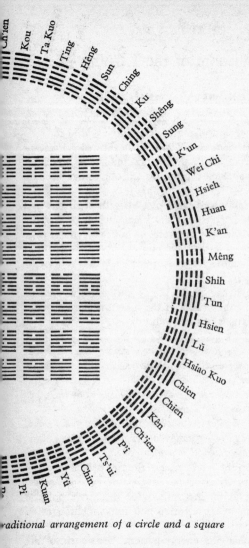

Ch'ien
Kou
Ta Kuo
Ting
Hêng
Sun
Ching
Ku
Shêng
Sung
K'un
Wei Chi
Hsieh
Huan
K'an
Mêng
Shih
Tun
Hsien
Lü
Hsiao Kuo
Chien
Chien
Kên
Ch'ien
Pi
Ts'ui
Chin
Yü
Kuan
Pi

raditional arrangement of a circle and a square

CHAPTER 3

The Wisdom of the I Ching

THE UNIVERSE IN MINIATURE

THE oracle embodies a simple yet profound explanation of the nature of the universe and of the life contained within it.

At the root of all existence lies *T'ai Chi*, the ultimate, unknowable source of life from which all things come and to which all things return. It embraces everything and all things encompass it.

The nearest we can approach T'ai Chi is through the one aspect of life which is constant: the phenomenon of change. Everything in the universe is in a state of flux; everything is in the process of changing into something else. Nothing is final; changes follow one another in a recurrent cycle and every end is also a beginning.

The processes of change can be seen everywhere: in the ebb and flow of the tides, the phases of the moon, the cycle of the seasons, and the fortunes of mankind.

One of the Confucian commentaries on the oracle, the *Great Appendix*, says: *The sun goes and the moon comes; the moon goes and the sun comes; sun and moon succeed each other, and their radiance is the outcome.*

Cold goes and heat comes; heat goes and cold comes; by this cycle of the cold and heat the year is completed.

That which is past becomes less and less, and that which lies ahead grows more and more; this contraction and expansion influence each other and advantageous progress is made.

Change arises from the interaction of the two primal forces of Yang and Yin, the positive and negative elements of existence. The complex interplay of energy between these two poles of manifestation results in the creation and transmutation of all things.

This constantly changing energy-pattern, the matrix of life itself, is called *Tao*, meaning the Way. Tao is the life-force, the power which underlies the forces of nature. By it all things are created and all things are dissolved.

From the opposing yet complementary concepts of Yin and Yang the originators of the I Ching evolved the eight trigrams to represent basic stages in the cycle of change. By combining the eight trigrams in pairs, sixty-four hexagrams were produced, each one revealing a minor phase in the cycle.

Later, each of the six lines of every hexagram was assigned a meaning of its own, thus offering the student a further 384 valuable pointers in the search for the secret of change.

The oracle was designed to reflect all levels of the process of transmutation in the universe; from creation through growth, maturity, decline, dissolution, and re-creation. It is a complete reflection of the natural order in miniature.

The Sage gazes up and contemplates the phenomena of the heavens, then looks down and examines the patterns of the earth; thereby he learns the causes of darkness and light.

He traces things to their beginning and follows them to their end; therefore he knows the significance of life and death.

He observes how the union of essence and breath form things, and how the disappearance of the Spirit produces their dissolution; therefore he knows the constitution of the lower and higher Souls.

THE ORACLE AND TIME: THE SEASONS

For over 3,000 years the I Ching has been used in China to reflect the cycle of the seasons and the yearly round of human activities.

The traditional Chinese calendar divides the year into two halves, the first six months being ruled by Yang, and the second six months by Yin. The new year commences in February, the month before the spring Equinox, and opens the six months of creative activity which come under the domination of the forces of Yang. During this time the masculine pursuits of farming, hunting, building, and marrying are all-important.

The Yang phase passes its peak in June, prior to the summer Solstice, and wanes until it is superseded by the forces of Yin, which begin their reign just before the autumn Equinox in September.

During the second half of the year more docile, feminine activities come to the fore: weaving, recreation, the planning of the year ahead, and childbirth.

The high-point of the Yin period is reached before the winter Solstice in December, after which the forces of Yang begin to reassert themselves, finally becoming predominant once more in February, the start of a new year.

Each of the twelve months of the year is ruled by a hexagram, called the *sovereign* hexagram. The twelve sovereign hexagrams illustrate the rise and fall of the forces of Yang and Yin through the year:

Yang:

Yin:

Knowing the correct attribution of these hexagrams can be of value in divination as an aid to discovering the most fortunate time to begin a project, bring some matter to a close, or fix the timing of some future event.

If timing is of importance in the question you are about to put to the oracle, the occurrence of one of these twelve hexagrams in the answer may be of great significance. But you must remember to take the complete answer into account; often the problem of correct timing is solved in the text accompanying a hexagram.

Here, as a guide, is an outline of the Chinese calendar. The months are traditionally divided into two fortnights, each of which has a title giving the main natural phenomena to be expected at that time of year.

It is said that these titles reflect the seasonal changes that take place in North China in a remarkably accurate fashion. They are given here because they reveal the recurrent cycle of Yang and Yin through the year in a clear and simple manner.

Month	Sovereign Hexagram	Names of the Fortnights	Commencing
1.	T'AI	Beginning of Spring	5 Feb.
		The Rains	20 Feb.
2.	TA CHUANG	Awakening of Creatures	7 March
		Spring Equinox	22 March
3.	KUAI	Clear and Bright	6 April
		Grain Rain	21 April
4.	CH'IEN	Beginning of Summer	6 May
		Lesser Fullness	22 May
5.	KOU	Grain in Ear	7 June
		Summer Solstice	22 June
6.	TUN	Lesser Heat	8 July
		Greater Heat	24 July
7.	P'I	Beginning of Autumn	8 Aug.
		End of Heat	24 Aug.
8.	KUAN	White Dews	8 Sept.
		Autumn Equinox	24 Sept.
9.	PO	Cold Dews	9 Oct.
		Descent of Hoar Frost	24 Oct.
10.	K'UN	Beginning of Winter	8 Nov.
		Lesser Snow	23 Nov.
11.	FU	Greater Snow	7 Dec.
		Winter Solstice	22 Dec.

THE SUPERIOR MAN

The I Ching teaches that events do not happen in an arbitrary, chaotic manner, but follow the immutable Way of Tao as revealed through the laws of change. All things are subject to change, but can only change in a certain way at any one time.

By knowing the stage that a particular cycle of change has reached, the oracle teaches that it is possible to predict the stage that must inevitably follow.

By applying this to the constantly altering conditions of one's own life the uncertainty of human existence can be avoided. Like the captain of a sailing ship, who by his knowledge of the tides and winds can turn them to his advantage and thus reach his chosen destination, so the person who turns to the Oracle of Change in times of doubt and indecision can chart a safe path through life.

Such an individual is described by the oracle as the *Superior Man*. The Great Commentary says: *When the superior man is about to take action of a private or a public nature he refers to the oracle, making his inquiry in words. It receives his message, and the answer comes as if it were an echo. Whether the subject be far or near, mysterious or profound, he knows forthwith what its outcome will be.*

The I Ching reveals that nothing stands still, nothing lasts for ever, and that for everything there is a proper time. He who does not strive to hasten good fortune prematurely, he who can accept inevitable decline, achieves true contentment; treading the middle path of balanced progress he avoids all conflict by aligning himself with the steady rhythms of nature, and finally becomes one with Tao.

He plans his life on the basis of the oracle's insight into the cycles of change. Aware that his smallest word or action creates ripples in the ocean of Tao which may have incalculable effects on his future, he proceeds with modesty and caution at all times: *Words issue from one's person, and proceed to influence the people.*

Actions proceed from what is near, and their effects are seen at a distance. Words and actions are the hinge and spring of the superior man. The movement of that hinge and spring determines glory or disgrace. His words and actions move heaven and earth; may he be careless of them?

The I Ching was created at a time when man's links with the deeper levels of his own psyche were stronger and clearer than they are today. It is a powerhouse of psychic images which can act as a bridge between our conscious minds and the depths of the unconscious.

That such a bridge is necessary is revealed by the inadequacy of the intellect to solve the fundamental problems of human existence. Science can show us how, but only intuition, the faculty of the unconscious, can tell us why.

The I Ching is the path which leads between the twin pillars of Yin and Yang through into the world where all is one and one is all; where tension is resolved and life is timeless: *When we investigate closely the nature and reasons of things, until we have entered into the inscrutable and spirit-like essence of them, we achieve the greatest practical use of them. When that use becomes swift and immediate, and personal tranquillity is secured, our virtue is thereby exalted.*

Proceeding beyond this, we reach a point which it is hardly possible to know. We have thoroughly comprehended the inscrutable and spirit-like, and know the processes of transformation; this is the fullness of virtue.

The superior man knows through his own experience that this is true; by willingly subordinating himself to the cosmic cycles of the universe he becomes master of his fate: *The superior man is he who in his qualities is in harmony with Heaven and Earth; in his brilliance with the sun and moon; in his orderly progress with the four seasons; and in his relations to what is fortunate and unfortunate, with the gods.*

He may precede Heaven and Heaven will not oppose him; he may follow Heaven, yet will only act as Heaven itself would act. If Heaven will not oppose him, how much less will man and the gods!

CHAPTER 4

How to Consult the Oracle

WHENEVER you want to consult the I Ching, set aside a little time during which you will not be disturbed to cast the hexagrams and interpret the result. Steady concentration is needed to calculate the lines of the hexagrams accurately, and at the same time you must try to keep your question clearly in your mind.

The wording of the question to be asked is also important. Try to phrase it in such a way that a definite answer is possible. If your problem is one of a choice to be made, for example 'Should I take job A or job B?' divide this question into two: 'What will be the likely outcome if I take job A?' Followed by: 'What will be the likely outcome if I take job B?' Then make your choice by comparing the two answers you receive.

If you want the answer to give some indication of time, include a time limit in the question. For example: 'Would I be wise to travel abroad during the next two weeks?' Or 'How will my new job go during the next three months?'

The I Ching's advice is extremely valuable when you are at the beginning of something new. At this stage you are still able to decide which way to go; control of the situation is largely in your own hands.

Armed with the oracle's guidance on future events and how best to cope with them, you are more likely to succeed than if you delay the consultation until a crisis threatens and drastic measures are needed if you are to be saved.

If the answer you receive to your question seems obscure or even irrelevant, don't dismiss it out of hand. Study it, and try to bear it in mind. It may slip into place quite suddenly, and awaken you to a quite startling insight into the true nature of your deepest difficulties – and how to solve them.

Often the I Ching seems to have the power to delve beneath the surface of immediate preoccupations and give advice on the more fundamental, long-term problems which lie buried. If we are unaware of our real problems, we are unlikely to see the significance of the answer to them at first glance.

If the advice you receive is not to your liking you can, of course, ignore it and go your own way. But repeated experiments over the centuries have taught many people that it is much better and ultimately more rewarding to accept it.

Traditionally, respect should be shown for the I Ching by looking after it reverently. The book should be kept wrapped in a piece of clean black silk, and resting on a shelf above shoulder height which faces north.

*

There are three methods of consulting the I Ching: the *Yarrow Stalk method*, the *Three Coins method*, and the *Six Wands method*.

Of these the oldest and most complicated, but undoubtedly the best, is the Yarrow Stalk method.

Divining with the yarrow sticks takes practice, some skill, and not a little patience; but the results are well worth the time and effort involved.

Consulting the Oracle of Change is a serious matter which should not be undertaken casually. It is one of those systems whereby the more concentration and work you put in, the better is the quality of the results that come out.

CASTING THE YARROW STALKS

Fifty yarrow stalks are traditionally required for this method. These are dried stalks of the common yarrow, or milfoil (*Achillea Millefolium*).

To the Chinese of ancient times the yarrow plant was considered sacred, being one of the 'Spirit-like' things possessed of a special virtue which suited it to divinatory use. Right up to the present century yarrow was faithfully planted on and around the grave of Confucius.

In practice narrow wooden sticks about twelve to eighteen inches in length seem to work very well; rods of $\frac{3}{16}''$ thick wooden dowel are readily obtainable and are easy to handle, while specially made divining sticks made of split bamboo which have a pleasant texture and feel about them can be bought.

The sticks should be placed carefully in a closed container when they are not in use, and kept alongside the Oracle.

Here is how you commence the consultation: unwrap the black silk cover from around the Oracle, spread it on a table and place the book on it. Stand before the book, facing north, and bow three times towards it.

Next a stick of incense should be lit and placed in a suitable receptacle on the table, and the yarrow stalks removed from their container.

During this ritual try to clear your mind of random thoughts and concentrate only on the question you want answered.

Now follow the instructions below carefully. Take your time, and don't worry if you get lost at some point to begin with. After you've done it a few times you will find yourself manipulating the stalks automatically, and you'll be able to put all your concentration to the problem in hand.

1 Take the bundle of stalks, remove one and place it back in the container. This stalk will take no further part in the inquiry. Its sole purpose is to bring the total number of stalks up to the magically significant number of 50.

2 Place the remaining 49 stalks in a heap before you.

3 Using your right hand, divide the stalks at random into two heaps, placing these a little apart.

4 Lift one stalk from the heap on the right with your right hand, and place it between the ring finger and the little finger of your left hand.

5 Now focus your attention on the left-hand heap. With your right hand, discard stalks from this heap, four stalks at a time, placing them together in one bundle to the left, until you are left with four or a lesser number of stalks.

6 Place these remaining stalks (or stalk) between the ring finger and middle finger of your left hand.

7 Now with your right hand discard stalks from the right hand heap four at a time, until four or less than four stalks are left.

8 Place these remaining stalks between the middle finger and index finger of your left hand.

9 Add the discarded stalks to the first lot of discarded stalks on the left.

You will now discover that you are holding between the fingers of your left hand a total of either 5 or 9 stalks ($1+1+3$, $1+3+1$, $1+2+2$, or $1+4+4$). Put these stalks carefully aside.

Now gather together all the stalks you had previously discarded. Using these stalks (49 less the 5 or 9 you have just put aside) begin the whole process again, beginning at stage (3), i.e.:

Take one stalk from the right-hand heap and place it between the ring and little finger of your left hand.

Discard stalks from the left-hand heap four at a time, until four or less than four are left.

Place these between the ring and middle fingers of your left hand.

Discard stalks from the right-hand heap four at a time until four or less are left.

Place these stalks between the middle and index finger of your left hand.

This time the number of stalks remaining in your left hand will be either 4 or 8 ($1+1+2$, $1+2+1$, $1+4+3$, or $1+3+4$).

Place these stalks near, but slightly apart from, the first heap of 5 or 9 stalks.

Gather the discarded stalks together once more; not, of course, including the two small heaps of 5 or 9 stalks, and 4 or 8 stalks.

Now begin the whole process again for the third time, starting with stage (3). Once again the number of stalks remaining at the end (stage 9) in your left hand, will number 4 or 8.

When this is completed you will have, beside the discarded stalks, three small heaps comprising 5 or 9 stalks, 4 or 8 stalks, and again 4 or 8 stalks. These will give you the *bottom* line of your hexagram.

Check the three numbers you have against the table below:

5+4+4	————O————	an Old Yang line
9+8+8	———X———	an Old Yin line
5+8+8 ⎫		
9+8+4 ⎬	—————————	a Young Yang line
9+4+8 ⎭		
5+4+8 ⎫		
5+8+4 ⎬	——— ———	a Young Yin line
9+4+4 ⎭		

As you will see, there are four possible lines that can occur. When you have discovered and noted down the line appropriate to your sequence of numbers, gather together the complete collection of 49 stalks, and go through the entire process again. This will give you the *second* line up from the bottom of your hexagram.

This whole procedure must be gone through a total of six times, until you have the six lines of a complete hexagram, starting at the bottom and working up to the top.

When you have a complete hexagram, collect the stalks together and put them away in their container.

Look at the lines making up the hexagram you have created and note if they are 'Old' or 'Young' lines. If the hexagram is formed only from Young Yang lines (—————————) and Young Yin lines (——— ———), just read the Decision, Commentary, and Image attached to it in the text. The interpretations given to the individual lines will not be relevant to your question.

If your hexagram includes any Old Yang lines (————O————) or Old Yin lines (——— X ———), you must read the passages given to those lines by the Duke of Chou, in addition to the main text.

These 'Old' lines are known also as 'moving' lines, because when they occur you can carry the reading a step further by changing them into their opposites:

————O———— (Old Yang) becomes ——— ——— (Young Yin), and ——— X ——— (Old Yin) becomes ————————— (Young Yang).

36

The process of 'moving the lines' will give you a new hexagram.

The main text, Decision, Commentary, and Image, of this new hexagram (but *not* the individual line meanings) will throw extra light on your question.

Each of the four types of line is given a traditional 'Ritual Number':

——— X ———   Ritual Number 6 (moving)

——————————   Ritual Number 7 (non-moving)

——— ———   Ritual Number 8 (non-moving)

———— O ————   Ritual Number 9 (moving)

This is why the Duke of Chou's comment on each line is prefixed by 'Six in the ... place', or 'Nine in the ... place'. Six and nine are the Ritual Numbers assigned to the two moving lines.

Here is an example of an I Ching consultation, which will show you the method of divining.

Assume that you have already asked your question and cast the yarrow stalks, gaining the following results:

Sixth line   5+8+8 =   ——————————

Fifth line   9+4+4 =   ——— ———

Fourth line   5+4+4 =   ————— O —————

Third line   9+4+8 =   ——————————

Second line   9+8+8 =   ——— X ———

First line   5+8+8 =   ——————————

The first hexagram you look up will be this one, Number 30:

LI, brilliant beauty

37

Locate this hexagram in the text by referring to the key on page 42. Study the Decision, Commentary, and Image, plus the Duke of Chou's words concerning lines two and four, which are moving lines.

Then transform the two moving lines of the hexagram into their opposites. Line two ——— X ——— becomes —————————, and line four ——— O ——— becomes ——— ———.

This gives you hexagram Number 26, TA CH'U, Accumulation through restraint:

Study the Decision, Commentary, and Image of this hexagram, but do not refer to the meanings of the lines.

Finally, recap what you have read and try to apply its several parts to your question. Often the reply will contain much that appears strange or irrelevant at first reading, but persevere and you will soon find that much of the oracle's advice is amazingly apt.

The I Ching is very ancient, and its sayings may not always appear on the surface to have much relevance to modern problems or the present-day world. To make the most of what the oracle has to offer you must first get the *feel* of the text as a whole, reading it slowly and allowing its rich imagery to flow into your subconscious mind.

Then read it through once more and try to grasp intuitively the message behind the words.

In time your familiarity with this technique will enable you to 'read between the lines' as it were, finding greater depths of meaning in the various passages as your understanding grows.

The oracle speaks to the older, deeper, less logical levels of the mind, and it is from these levels that enlightenment will come.

If you find a sharp distinction between the meanings of the text of a hexagram and the meanings of its moving lines, this signifies that the main answer to your question will be adapted in some way by special events or circumstances.

If you find that a second hexagram contradicts the first, the earlier hexagram refers to events nearer at hand, and the second hexagram to later developments of a contrary nature.

THROWING THE THREE COINS

The three coins method is much simpler than the older yarrow stalk method. All one has to do is toss three coins into the air a few times and note how they fall in order to arrive at a hexagram without much effort.

Traditionally the correct coins to use for this are the old bronze Chinese coins which are inscribed on one side only and have a hole in the middle. However, these are not easily found nowadays and you will probably have to resort to the use of modern coins.

To begin you need three coins of the same size and denomination. Decide which side of the coin represents the inscribed side of the old Chinese coins. Generally the side that gives the value of the coin is chosen.

Shake the three coins loosely together between your hands, then drop them on to a smooth, level surface.

Note which way up each coin falls.

The inscribed side of each coin counts as 2, and the reverse side as 3.

Therefore, three inscribed sides together equal 6, the Ritual Number of an Old Yin line ——— X ———.

Three reverse sides together equal 9, the Ritual Number of an Old Yang line. ——————O——————

Two inscribed sides and one reverse side equal 7, the Ritual Number of a Young Yang line ————————.

Two reverse sides and one inscribed side equal 8, the Ritual Number of a Young Yin line ——— ———.

The way the three coins fall gives you the *bottom* line of your hexagram.

Shake and drop the coins again to obtain the second line up from the bottom, and continue in this way until you have six lines.

Interpret the hexagram (or hexagrams if the first one contains one or more 'moving lines') as described in the section on yarrow stalk divination, on pages 36–9 inclusive.

THE SIX WANDS METHOD

The six wands method is the simplest of all; you merely roll the six inscribed wands on to a table and note how they fall, giving you a complete hexagram at once. It is probably the best system to start with; as you become more familiar with the structure and terminology of the I Ching you can graduate to the more complex methods.

For this method you need to acquire or make a set of six special wands.

These should be about 8″ by 1″ in size, and $\frac{1}{8}$″ thick. The traditional sets were often made of valuable materials such as ivory, tortoise-shell, or rare woods, but you can easily make a set from strips of ordinary wood of the appropriate size.

Each wand should be painted black on both sides, with a $1\frac{1}{2}$″-wide band of white painted across one side in the middle.

The six wands are therefore Yang lines ——————— when facing all-black side up, and Yin lines ——— ——— when the white band is showing.

All that is necessary to obtain a quick answer to your question is to shuffle the six wands out of sight (behind your back is the best place), then roll them on to a table in front of you as if you were unrolling a small mat.

Starting with the wand that lies nearest to you, pick them up and arrange them in the form of a hexagram. The nearest wand will form the bottom line of the hexagram, the next nearest will form the second line up, and so on.

Look up the hexagram in the key to the hexagrams on page 42, read the Decision, Commentary, and Image, and you have the answer to your question.

This is the simplest and quickest method of consulting the I Ching. But the answer to your question will be confined to the text of *one* hexagram. As you can have no 'moving lines', the words of the Duke of Chou on the several lines cannot be used, and for the same reason the hexagram you get cannot be expanded into a second hexagram.

Use the six wands method to begin with if you don't feel ready to tackle the mysteries of the 'moving lines', or if you are very pressed for time, but remember that its usefulness is limited.

If the I Ching is to be allowed to function at its best you must be prepared to work at it. By all means start with the six wands, but always let your aim be mastery of the yarrow stalks.

*

Here is a key to locating the hexagrams. Look for the upper trigram in the top, horizontal column, and then find the lower trigram in the far left vertical column. Read down from the upper trigram and across from the lower trigram until the two meet. The number given at this point is the number of your hexagram.

For example, if the hexagram you wanted to locate was:

you would locate ▬▬▬ in the horizontal column, and ▬ ▬ in the vertical column. Cross reference from these two points gives you the number 37, the number of your hexagram.

UPPER TRIGRAM / LOWER TRIGRAM	Ch'ien	Chên	K'an	Kên	K'un	Sun	Li	Tui
Ch'ien	1	34	5	26	11	9	14	43
Chên	25	51	3	27	24	42	21	17
K'an	6	40	29	4	7	59	64	47
Kên	33	62	39	52	15	53	56	31
K'un	12	16	8	23	2	20	35	45
Sun	44	32	48	18	46	57	50	28
Li	13	55	63	22	36	37	30	49
Tui	10	54	60	41	19	61	38	58

Key to locating the hexagrams in the text

CHAPTER 5

Introduction to the Oracle

READING THE TEXT OF THE I CHING

EACH of the sixty-four hexagrams has several explanatory texts attached to it. All these texts add something of value to the overall message of the hexagram.

The first, and oldest, text is called the Decision (*T'uan* in Chinese). This is King Wên's own concise interpretation of the hexagram's basic meaning.

The second text is made up of later Confucian commentaries on the Decision. It expands and discusses King Wên's interpretation.

The third text is called the Image (*Hsiang*) and relates the hexagram to human affairs. It suggests how one should act by describing how the superior man would proceed in such circumstances.

These three texts complete the remarks on the hexagram as a whole.

The fourth text is made up of the Duke of Chou's interpretations of the six lines. These short passages (called *Yao*) are frequently rather mysterious and difficult to link with the general meaning of the hexagram.

The fifth and final text is a commentary on the Duke of Chou's words. The interpretation and commentary relating to the moving lines need to be studied carefully. They speak in the language of the unconscious, and are best understood by one's intuition rather than one's intellect.

KEY PHRASES IN THE I CHING

You will find as you refer to the oracle that certain passages occur again and again. These are generally of great importance, and contain the essence of the oracle's message. Here is a list of the more important key phrases, with indications of how they should be interpreted.

Supreme success: The complete fulfilment of your hopes. This phrase implies that your actions are fully in harmony with the prevailing cycles of Tao.

Advantage will come from being firm and correct: Satisfactory progress is possible, but you must persevere and proceed along a course which accords with the Will of Heaven. What this course is will generally be revealed in the description of the superior man's actions.

Crossing the Great Water: This can refer to a journey overseas, but also applies to the successful overcoming of any major obstacle. In the days when the I Ching was composed, the 'Great Water' was the river Yangtse, a wide and swift-flowing body of water which would only be crossed on important occasions.

The superior man: He whose actions are in complete accord with Tao. The I Ching offers him as a model of supreme wisdom and virtue.

The great man: Although sometimes used as a synonym for the superior man, this generally refers to someone in a position of influence and authority who can help or hinder you.

The sage: Greater than the superior man, he has reached at-one-ment with Tao, and is therefore incapable of human error.

No error: Although events may not turn out in the way you hope, you are following a correct course of action and ultimate success will be yours.

Firm persistence: You should persevere against all odds.

Misfortune: Continuing along your present course will have an unfortunate outcome. You should apply your efforts elsewhere.

There will be evil: You are in a very dangerous situation; quick action is needed if disaster is to be avoided.

Occasion to repent: If you proceed as you intend, you will regret having done so.

Peril: Conditions around you require handling with extreme care.

Blame: If you proceed, you will not only fail but will suffer a serious loss of prestige as well.

No blame: You may fail, but will not be criticized for having done so.

No advantage: Perseverance will be of no avail. You should abandon your efforts.

THE SIXTY-FOUR HEXAGRAMS

Below is a list of the sixty-four hexagrams in the order in which they appear in the text. Alongside each hexagram you will find its name, followed by a guide to pronouncing the name, then its meaning.

The Wade system of transliterating Chinese sounds into English has been used in this book, because it is the system most widely known in English-speaking parts of the world.

However, the way in which words are spelt in this system does not correspond exactly with the way they are pronounced; the system was originally designed for international usage and therefore employs some non-English sounds.

In order to help readers who are unfamiliar with Chinese pronunciation, the name of each hexagram is given first according to Wade, then spelt as closely as possible to the way it is spoken.

In some of the names the vowel is so short as to be almost silent. In such cases the vowel has been omitted in the phonetic spelling, its place being indicated by an apostrophe. For example, hexagram 32 is entitled *Hêng* in the Wade system, and is spelt *H'ng* phonetically to indicate the almost silent vowel.

A further non-English sound is that of the final letter ü, which occurs in the names of hexagrams 5 (Hsü), 10 (Lü), 16 (Yü), and 56 (Lü). These names are all pronounced to rhyme with the French pronoun 'Tu'.

All the other names should be pronounced as they are spelt phonetically.

THE HEXAGRAMS

No.	Hexagram	Name	Pronunciation	Meaning
1.		CH'IEN	Chee-en	Creativity
2.		K'UN	Kw'n	Quiescence
3.		CHUN	Jw'n	Birth Pangs
4.		MÊNG	M'ng	Inexperience
5.		HSÜ	Shu	Biding One's Time
6.		SUNG	Soong	Strife
7.		SHIH	Shrr	The Army
8.		PI	Bee	Unity
9.		HSIAO CH'U	She-aw Choo	Restraint by the Weak
10.		LÜ	Lu	Treading
11.		T'AI	Tie	Peace
12.		P'I	Pee	Stagnation

No.	Hexagram	Name	Pronunciation	Meaning
13.		T'UNG JÊN	Toong R'n	Fellowship
14.		TA YU	Da You	Wealth
15.		CH'IEN	Chee-en	Modesty
16.		YÜ	Yu	Calm Confidence
17.		SUI	Sway	Following
18.		KU	Goo	Decay
19.		LIN	Lin	Getting Ahead
20.		KUAN	Gwun	Contemplation
21.		SHIH HO	Shrr Huh	Biting Through
22.		PI	Bee	Adornment
23.		PO	Po (as in *upon*)	Shedding
24.		FU	Foo	Returning

No.	Hexagram	Name	Pronunciation	Meaning
25.		WU WANG	Woo Wung	Simple Integrity
26.		TA CH'U	Da Choo	Accumulation through Restraint
27.		I	Yee	Nourishment
28.		TA KUO	Da Gwoh	Excess
29.		K'AN	Kun	The Perilous Chasm
30.		LI	Lee	Brilliant Beauty
31.		HSIEN	Shee-en	Mutual Attraction
32.		HÊNG	H'ng	Long Duration
33.		TUN	Dun	Withdrawal
34.		TA CHUANG	Da Jwung	Vigorous Strength
35.		CHIN	Jin	Progress
36.		MING I	Ming Yee	Hiding of the Light
37.		CHIA JÊN	Jeeah R'n	The Family

No.	Hexagram	Name	Pronunciation	Meaning
38.		K'UEI	Kway	Opposites
39.		CHIEN	Jee-en	Obstructions
40.		HSIEH	Shee-ay	Escape
41.		SUN	Sun	Decrease
42.		I	Yee	Increase
43.		KUAI	Gwy	Renewed Advance
44.		KOU	Go	Sudden Encounters
45.		TS'UI	Tsway	Collecting Together
46.		SHÊNG	Sh'ng	Ascending
47.		K'UN	Kw'n	Exhausting Restriction
48.		CHING	Jing	The Well
49.		KÔ	Guh	Revolution
50.		TING	Ding	The Cauldron

No.	Hexagram	Name	Pronunciation	Meaning
51.		CHÊN	J'n	Thunder
52.		KÊN	G'n	Stillness
53.		CHIEN	Jee-en	Gradual Advance
54.		KUEI MEI	Gway May	The Marrying Maiden
55.		FÊNG	F'ng	Abundant Prosperity
56.		LÜ	Lu	The Travelling Stranger
57.		SUN	Sun	Gentle Penetration
58.		TUI	Dway	Joy
59.		HUAN	Hwun	Dispersion
60.		CHIEH	Jee-eh	Regulation
61.		CHUNG FU	Joong Foo	Inmost Sincerity
62.		HSIAO KUO	Shee-aw Gwoh	Small Successes
63.		CHI CHI	Jee Jee	Completion Achieved
64.		WEI CHI	Way Jee	Before Completion

Part Two: The Text of the I Ching

Hexagram 1

CH'IEN

CREATIVITY

The trigrams: CH'IEN: Heaven, active. CH'IEN: Heaven, active.

THE DECISION

Creativity. Supreme success. Perseverance in the right way brings good fortune.

COMMENTARY

Great is the power of primal creativity (Ch'ien). The source of all things, it embodies the significance of Heaven. Clouds move and rain falls, and all things develop in their appropriate forms.

Sages comprehend the relationship between the end and the beginning, and how the lines of the hexagram reach completion, each in its season. Mounting them at the appropriate time, they drive through the heavens as though drawn by six dragons.

Creativity changes and transforms, in order that everything might attain its true nature in accordance with the will of Heaven. Great harmony can then prevail. Firm correctness furthers.

The Sage appears on high, bringing peace to every realm.

By acting in accordance with the rhythm of the universe one's aspirations are fulfilled; great achievements are only possible when the right time has come. Time is not an enemy to be vanquished, but an ally who must be worked with patiently.

The superior man strives to align himself with the set of the celestial tides, thus attracting good fortune and supreme success.

THE LINES

Nine in the first place: The dragon lies hidden in the deep. This is not the time to act.

The dragon appears in the field

Interpretation: One should be as a dragon lying hidden in the depths of the water; that is, carefully conserving one's energy while observing the progress of events and preparing to act when the right moment occurs.

Nine in the second place: The dragon appears in the field. It will be advantageous to meet the great man.
Interpretation: Like a dragon appearing in a field, the great man reveals himself to the world. It favours one to become acquainted with such a man.

Nine in the third place: The superior man is active all day, and remains vigilant in the evening. Danger surrounds him, but he will make no mistake.

Interpretation: His position is vulnerable, therefore he should exercise vigilance while actively improving his circumstances by day, and remain aware of the dangers around him even by night.

Nine in the fourth place: The dragon seems on the point of springing upwards, but remains still in the deep. There will be no mistake.

Interpretation: The superior man observes the situation without committing himself. This is a fortunate time for making long-term plans.

Nine in the fifth place: The dragon is on the wing, flying across the sky. It will be advantageous to meet the great man.

Interpretation: The time is auspicious for casting off caution and openly allying oneself with a great man, he whose aims are akin to one's own.

Nine in the sixth place: The reckless dragon will have cause for remorse.

Interpretation: He is in danger of failing through over-ambition. The superior man knows when to retreat as well as when to advance; when to grasp and when to release; when to conquer and when to set free.

Hexagram 2

K'UN

QUIESCENCE

The trigrams: K'UN: Earth, responsive. K'UN: Earth, responsive.

THE DECISION

Quiescence. Supreme success. Like the mare which is strong, steadfast, and docile, the superior man does not take the initiative but faithfully serves those who can best use his talents. There will be advantage in finding friends in the south and west, and in losing friends in the north and east. In quiet persistence lies good fortune.

COMMENTARY

Great is the power of Quiescence (K'un). It obediently receives the forces of creativity, and all things owe their birth to it.

It enfolds everything in its embrace, and complements the unlimited power of creativity. Through its shining abundance all things are able to reach their full development.

The mare is both docile and strong, and fitted for the service of man. The quiet strength of the mare symbolizes the earth, just as the active creativity of the dragon symbolizes Heaven.

The superior man, like the mare, finds a true master, and chooses his friends among those whose natures are compatible with his own. In his quiescence lies his strength. The persistence indicated here is of a passive earthly nature, like that of the mare.

THE IMAGE

K'un symbolizes the receptive power of the earth. The superior man supports all things by his virtue.

THE LINES

Six in the first place: Treading on hoarfrost. Solid ice is coming.
Interpretation: A time of danger is about to commence. When a man walks on hoarfrost, great caution and delicacy of movement is needed. The wise man knows that hoarfrost is followed in due course by thick ice and makes his plans accordingly. Such foresight is needed at this time.

Six in the second place: Being straight, square and great, its purpose will be effortlessly advantageous.
Interpretation: The natural order is straightforward, unhurried, yet great. Without effort everything is brought to a successful conclusion. The superior man takes nature as his model: he is open in his dealings, calm in his actions, and thus without strain he attains greatness.

Six in the third place: He restrains his excellence, yet firmly maintains it. If engaged in the king's service he brings his duties to a successful conclusion, yet does not claim credit for himself.
Interpretation: The superior man does not boast of his talent, but applies it to the best advantage. When employed by a superior he works quietly in the background and lets the credit go to the one above him. In this way success comes to him effortlessly.

Six in the fourth place: A sack tied up. No ground for blame or for praise.
Interpretation: Like a sack which is firmly tied up, one should keep one's valuables hidden in times of danger. Such prudence

will foil the designs of ambitious enemies, and also keep one from depending on the good will of others.

Six in the fifth place. The yellow undergarment. There will be no great good fortune.
Interpretation: The superior man is humble; he does not display his virtues directly as if he were wearing an undergarment of Imperial yellow colour, but lets them be revealed naturally through his conduct.

Sixth in the sixth place: Dragons fighting in the wilderness. Their blood is purple and yellow.
Interpretation: If one becomes discontented and seeks to assert oneself, a great battle with a superior will ensue. When two dragons fight in the wilderness, only bloodshed can be the result of such ill-judgement.

(Note: Purple and yellow are the sacred colours of earth and Heaven; when earth tries to usurp the position of Heaven, both suffer.)

Hexagram 3

CHUN

BIRTH PANGS

The trigrams: K'AN: Water, dangerous. CHÊN: Thunder,
arousing.

THE DECISION

Birth pangs. Great progress and success. Advantage will come
from being firm and correct, but any forward movement should
not be undertaken lightly. There will be advantage in appointing princes.

COMMENTARY

When the strong (Chên) and the weak (K'an) begin to unite, the
difficulties of birth will follow. The start of a new venture is
always accompanied by struggles and difficulty, and can only be
successful if one is patient and persevering.

In such a way the plant struggles with difficulty up out of the
earth, gradually rising above the surface as its persistence is
rewarded.

Such a task of creating order out of chaos should not be
begun in a frivolous manner, and it would be of advantage to
appoint competent helpers.

THE IMAGE

The combination of clouds (K'an) and thunder (Chên) signifies
birth pangs. The superior man accordingly sorts out the
material at hand and produces order from disorder.

Nine in the first place: Difficulty in advancing. Advantage will come from being firm and correct, and in appointing princes.
Interpretation: Obstacles lie ahead, but careful preparation and a slow advance will make it possible for them to be surmounted. It would be wise to appoint responsible assistants.

Six in the second place: He is in difficulties and obliged to turn back, retreating with his carriage and horses. The maiden is harassed by one who would make her his wife, but if she behaves firmly, in the correct manner, she will decline his offer. After ten years have passed she will marry and bear children.
Interpretation: Any attempt to move forward will end in distress and retreat. An offer of help from an unexpected and suspect quarter is better refused. Acceptable assistance which will ensure success will come when the time is right.

Six in the third place: He hunts deer without the help of a forester, and finds himself lost in the middle of the forest. The superior man, aware of the risk he is courting, chooses to give up the chase. To go forward would bring regret.
Interpretation: Successful progress cannot be sustained. An experienced guide is needed, and as such is not available it is advisable to abandon one's plan.

Six in the fourth place: The horses of her carriage retreat and she is unable to control them. She seeks the help of he who would make her his wife. The outcome will be fortunate and she will be able to proceed once more.
Interpretation: The situation is out of control, but help is available. This should be accepted, even if a certain loss of face is unavoidable.

Nine in the fifth place: He finds difficulty in dispensing the rich favours that are expected of him. Correct action will ensure good fortune in small things, but in great matters it will lead to disaster.

Interpretation: He is in a position of authority and strength, and is therefore expected to dispense favours on a large scale. But time is needed to consolidate what has been gained; great enterprises should not yet be attempted.

Six in the sixth place: He is obliged to fall back, taking his carriage and horses with him. Streams of blood and tears fall from him.
Interpretation: Failure lies ahead. A retreat is inevitable and despair will follow.

Hexagram 4

MÊNG

INEXPERIENCE

The trigrams: KÊN: Mountain, immovable. K'AN: Water, dangerous.

THE DECISION

Inexperience. There will be progress and success. I do not seek the youthful and inexperienced, but they seek me. A sincere and humble approach will incline me to give instruction, but if this is followed by a later falling away, then further applications will be too much trouble for me to concern myself with. Perseverance is necessary. However, even intermittent progress will resolve itself in eventual success.

COMMENTARY

At the foot of the mountain (Kên) lies a dangerous, water-filled chasm (K'an). This suggests the foolish stubbornness of youthful inexperience.

The inexperience of youth is rather like the undeveloped appearance of a plant which has just succeeded in struggling from beneath the surface of the earth. Such a state is not in itself evil, but needs the care and supervision of a competent teacher if it is to be successfully overcome. Also the eager co-operation of the subject is necessary.

THE IMAGE

The superior man strives to conduct himself in a resolute manner, and nourishes his virtue as if it were a spring at the foot of a mountain.

THE LINES

Six in the first place: Punishment is advantageous when used for the dispelling of ignorance, the removal of shackles from the mind. But an excess of punishment will lead to regret.
Interpretation: Discipline is necessary if one is to learn; punishment is sometimes needed to overcome stubborn ignorance. But this must not be overdone.

Nine in the second place: Exercising forbearance when dealing with the ignorant will lead to good fortune. Handling women in a kindly fashion will be fortunate. By observing such rules a son will be able to control his family.
Interpretation: Tolerance and the ability to discern good qualities in lowly people are characteristics which fit one for bearing the burden of public office.

Six in the third place: Do not marry a maiden who, when she sees a wealthy man, cannot keep herself from him. Nothing of advantage can come from her.
Interpretation: One should guard against marrying a woman whose ignorance causes her judgement to be impaired by a display of wealth.

Six in the fourth place: He is bound in his ignorance as if by chains. There will be occasion for regret.
Interpretation: Stubborn refusal to cast off ignorance will end in failure. But sometimes this painful process is a necessary part of the pupil's progress.

Six in the fifth place: The youthful innocent. There will be good fortune.

Interpretation: Good fortune will come to the youth who has no experience but who wisely seeks instruction.

Nine in the sixth place: He smites the ignorant youth, but no advantage can come from injuring him. Advantage can only come from keeping injury from him.

Interpretation: Rather than continuing to inflict punishment for stubborn ignorance beyond the point where it can do any good, one should become aware of the effect such violence has upon oneself and one's relationship with the pupil.

Hexagram 5

HSÜ

BIDING ONE'S TIME

The trigrams: K'AN: Water, dangerous. CH'IEN: Heaven, active.

THE DECISION

Biding one's time. Sincerity will lead to brilliant success. Firmness will bring good fortune. It will be advantageous to cross the great water.

COMMENTARY

Peril (K'an) lies ahead, but despite the urge towards activity (Ch'ien) which is shown, he will not allow himself to be involved in a dangerous situation.

Firm persistence in a right course of action will ensure great success. But strength and determination are needed to make the most of the progressive trends now operating. It is an auspicious time to commence a major undertaking.

The strong man's inclination when faced with danger is to advance on it and combat it without delay; but here one would be wise to wait until success is assured.

THE IMAGE

Clouds drift across the sky as if biding their time. The superior man, in accordance with this, eats and drinks, feasts and enjoys himself.

Nine in the first place: He waits on the border. If he constantly maintains his purpose there will be no error.

Interpretation: Calm inaction is the best policy at this time. By keeping his ultimate purpose in mind while remaining inactive, he will avoid provoking premature opposition to his plans.

Nine in the second place: He waits on the sand by a mountain stream. He will be injured by gossip directed against him, but in the end there will be good fortune.

Interpretation: Standing on the brink of a major endeavour, as if poised by the edge of a rushing stream, he will be the target of harmful criticism. Despite this, his ultimate success is assured.

Nine in the third place: He waits in the mud at the edge of the stream. He invites the approach of evil.

Interpretation: He is not in a sufficiently strong position to hazard a major leap forward.

Six in the fourth place: He waits, surrounded by blood. But he will escape from the chasm.

Interpretation: A fight to the death is imminent. This cannot be evaded, but firm resolution will give him the victory.

Nine in the fifth place: He stands waiting in the midst of a feast. Through his firm correctness there will be good fortune.

Interpretation: One should take advantage of the lull between battles to renew one's strength through feasting and laughter; but the serious business in hand must always be kept firmly in mind.

Six in the sixth place: He enters into the chasm. Three uninvited guests come. If he treats them with respect, the outcome will be fortunate.

Interpretation: The battle commences and he appears about to be overwhelmed. But unsolicited help is on the way; if he has the sense to accept it graciously he will be delivered from danger.

Hexagram 6

STRIFE

The trigrams: CH'IEN: Heaven, active. K'AN: Water, dangerous.

THE DECISION

Strife. Although sincere, he will be opposed and obstructed. If he acts with great caution there will be good fortune, but if he proceeds on his present course there will be evil. It will be advantageous to see the great man, but not to cross the great water.

COMMENTARY

The upper trigram of Sung represents strength (Chi'en) and the lower trigram represents danger (K'an). The coming together of strength and danger results in strife.

Although he is sincere and believes himself to be in the right, perseverance can only lead to conflict. The great man remains calm and ready to negotiate, prepared to submit his case to a higher authority and trust in justice being done. He would be foolish to begin a great enterprise at this time.

THE IMAGE

Heaven and water repel each other, leading to strife. The superior man considers his first steps when about to begin any transaction.

Six in the first place: He does not proceed. He will be spoken against, but the end will be fortunate.

Interpretation: Abandoning his present course will entail a loss of popularity, but the ultimate outcome will be favourable.

Nine in the second place: He is unequal to the conflict ahead. If he returns home the people of his city will remain free from harm.

Interpretation: His present resources are inadequate. Retiring gracefully to a place of safety will save him and his dependents from a damaging conflict.

Six in the third place: He keeps firmly in the place which is his by right. His position is perilous, but there will be good fortune in the end. If he engages in the service of the king he will not be awarded the merit he deserves.

Interpretation: A precarious situation should not impel one to act in haste; remaining secure in an assured position will lead to good fortune. Seeking an important assignment for the prestige it will bring will end in disappointment.

Nine in the fourth place: Unequal to the task before him, he retires and studies the way of Heaven, changing his aspirations and quietly resting in an attitude of firm persistence. There will be good fortune.

Interpretation: Heavy-handed pursuit of a fixed objective will lead to strife. Good fortune can still be attained by a re-examination of motives, followed by a redirection of effort in a sensitive and harmonious fashion.

Nine in the fifth place: He goes forth into battle. Great good fortune!

Interpretation: Unwavering pursuit of an objective will lead to great success. Prevailing conditions favour vigorous action.

Nine in the sixth place: The leather belt of honour is bestowed on him by the sovereign; but it is taken from him again three times in one day.

Interpretation: Unrelenting struggle will lead to victory and honour, but this will not last. Its benefits will be fleeting while opposition will still persist.

Hexagram 7

THE ARMY

The trigrams: K'UN: Earth, responsive. K'AN: Water, dangerous.

THE DECISION

The army. With firm correctness and an experienced leader there will be good fortune and no error.

COMMENTARY

The unbroken line in the centre of the lower trigram symbolizes strength, and the other lines respond to it. Firm action gives rise to danger, but people respond to it. Such action distresses the entire country, but the people will follow him who instigates it; with such good fortune, what error can there be?

An old, experienced leader who can impose firm discipline on those beneath him will gain the support of all, both high and low. But such a position of strength should not lead to an abuse of power; firmness and correct principles should motivate all actions.

A war should only be fought with a righteous end in mind. Furthermore, it should be conducted in the right manner, especially at the outset.

THE IMAGE

Water (K'an) in the midst of the earth (K'un). The superior man nourishes and educates the people, collecting a strong army of followers around him as a result.

Six in the first place: The army proceeds according to its orders. If these are not wise, there will be evil.

Interpretation: An army which goes forth into battle must know the cause for which it is fighting, and have a workable strategy at its command. Otherwise all will end in defeat.

The leader is in the midst of the army

Nine in the second place: The leader is in the midst of the army. There will be good fortune and no error. Three times the king honours him with decorations.

Interpretation: The good general is seen in the midst of his troops, where he can best direct them, and where they can be inspired by his presence.

Six in the third place: The army has many inefficient leaders. There will be evil.

Interpretation: If command is divided among many, strength and unity of direction are sure to be lost. The outcome will be disastrous.

Sixth in the fourth place: The army retreats. There is no error.
Interpretation: Disciplined retreat in the face of a superior force is not a sign of weakness; being the correct course of action in the circumstances it is a sign of strong leadership.

Six in the fifth place: There are birds in the fields. If they are seized and destroyed there will be no error. If the eldest son leads the army, and the youngest is fit only for removing corpses, there will be evil.
Interpretation: Marauders must be destroyed as if they were birds attacking the fields. An experienced general must be chosen to carry out the mission; younger men would prolong the conflict needlessly if allowed to gain command.

Six in the sixth place: The great ruler proclaims his edicts, appointing heads of states and heads of clans. Small men should not be employed in such positions.
Interpretation: The victorious prince rewards those who have gained the victory for him. To those who have shown themselves to be responsible he allocates positions of power and authority, while to lesser men he gives rewards which they cannot abuse.

Hexagram 8

UNITY

The trigrams: K'AN: Water, dangerous. K'UN: Earth,
responsive.

THE DECISION

Unity. Good fortune. Let him re-examine himself by means of
the oracle to see if he is virtuous, persistent, and firm in his
aims. If the answer is favourable there will be no error. Those
who are troubled will come to him; late-comers will encounter
misfortune.

COMMENTARY

Unity signifies good fortune through co-operation; in the hexagram we see inferiors (the broken lines) docilely following their
superior (the unbroken fifth line).

Good fortune is indicated, but a careful assessment of his
capabilities is first needed if error is to be avoided. This done,
those who now hesitate will gather round in support. Any who
delay too long will not share in the general good fortune.

THE IMAGE

Water (K'an) is over the earth (K'un). The ancient kings, in
accordance with this, established the various states and maintained affectionate relations with their governors.

Six in the first place: He seeks by means of his sincerity to achieve unity with those around him. There will be no error. Let his breast be as full of sincerity as an earthenware vessel is of its contents, and further advantage will be drawn to him. Interpretation: By showing sincerity in all his actions he will attain success. If his motives are totally sincere, unexpected good luck will follow.

Six in the second place: The movement towards unity proceeds from the inward mind. With firm persistence there will be good fortune.
Interpretation: When seeking to gain a closer understanding with others one should follow the direction of one's heart. Perseverance in the right way will lead to good fortune.

Six in the third place: He seeks union with those who should not be associated with.
Interpretation: If he seeks closer ties with those whose aims are incompatible with his own, no good can come of his efforts.

Six in the fourth place: He seeks for union with one beyond himself. With firm persistence there will be good fortune.
Interpretation: Working in an honest manner towards the achievement of closer links with superiors will be fortunate.

Nine in the fifth place: Holding together. The king urges pursuit of the game on three sides only, allowing all the animals to escape before him. The townspeople do not warn one another to prevent this. There will be good fortune.
Interpretation: He cannot achieve success alone. Like a king who pursues game which is hemmed in on three sides, yet who allows his prey to escape because the people ahead were not warned to stand guard, he must let his aims be known if essential co-operation is to be obtained. Yet the strength of this line is such that ultimate success is bound to come.

Six in the sixth place: He seeks unity, but has not taken the first steps towards achieving it. There will be evil.

Interpretation: Only failure can result from trying to unite those around without having first prepared the way and provided firm leadership.

Hexagram 9

HSIAO CH'U

RESTRAINT BY THE WEAK

The trigrams: SUN: Wind, gentle. CH'IEN: Heaven, active.

THE DECISION

Restraint by the weak. There will be no progress and success. We see dense clouds, but no rain coming from the western borders.

COMMENTARY

Here a broken line occupies the ruling position, and the unbroken lines above and below respond to it. It indicates strength combined with gentleness. A strong line occupies the centre of each trigram, showing that there will be progress and success.

The strong (Ch'ien) is gently restrained by the weak (Sun). There will be progress and ultimate success, but delay in the meantime is unavoidable. Docility and a flexible outlook will help. It is as if one waiting for rain sees dense clouds massing in the west, and knows that what he awaits is at last approaching.

THE IMAGE

The wind wafts across the sky. The superior man displays his virtue for all to see.

THE LINES

Nine in the first place: He returns and pursues his own path. How can he be mistaken? There will be good fortune.

Interpretation: If when stepping forward one is faced with a major obstacle, the wise course is to retreat to one's former position until a way round can be devised. Such self-restraint will lead to success.

Nine in the second place: He is persuaded into returning to his proper course. There will be good fortune.
Interpretation: The time is not auspicious for successful progress. He should retreat in the company of like-minded people.

Nine in the third place: The spokes of the carriage wheel are missing. Husband and wife stand looking with averted eyes.
Interpretation: Conditions are unfavourable for moving ahead or reaching agreements. Attempts to progress will lead to blame and embarrassment.

Six in the fourth place: He possesses sincerity. Because of this the danger of bloodshed is averted and his apprehension proved groundless. There will be no error.
Interpretation: Acting with self-confidence and obvious sincerity, even though fearing the outcome, will avert disaster.

Nine in the fifth place: Possessing sincerity, he draws others to him. Rich in resources, he binds his neighbours to him.
Interpretation: Observing sincerity in a person, people will draw round and pool their resources to serve the common cause.

Nine in the sixth place: The rain falls and progress is halted. Virtue accumulates. Firm persistence brings the woman into a position of peril, like the moon approaching to the full. If the superior man persists in his efforts at such a time, there will be evil.
Interpretation: The rain has fallen; success has been attained in fair measure. But when the moon becomes full, waning must follow. If he persists in his efforts beyond the time for resting, there is a danger that his gains will be lost. Docility and restraint are recommended.

Hexagram 10

LÜ

TREADING

The trigrams: CH'IEN: Heaven, active. TUI: Lake, joyful.

THE DECISION

Treading. He treads on the tail of a tiger, but it does not bite him. There will be progress and success.

COMMENTARY

Here the weak treads on the strong (in the lower trigram). The lower trigram indicates joy and satisfaction, and responds to the upper trigram indicating strength.

Dangerous and unpredictable people cannot harm him who treads carefully and gently as he moves forward. Observing the rules of propriety, one may safely tread amid scenes of disorder and peril.

The weak stands above the strong, but because it is done gently, in a courteous manner, there is no harm and the action is blameless.

THE IMAGE

Heaven (Ch'ien) is above, the lake (Tui) below. The superior man discriminates between high and low, and considers the aims of the people.

Nine in the first place: He treads his accustomed path. If he proceeds, there will be no error.

Interpretation: Treading a safe, accustomed path, taking on no extra obligations, will keep him out of dangerous situations.

Nine in the second place: He treads the path that is level and easy. A quiet and solitary man; if he be firm and correct, there will be good fortune.

Great caution is required of him who deliberately treads on a tiger's tail

Interpretation: Good fortune is attained by the hermit who acts with restraint, wisely keeping to the middle of the road.

Six in the third place: A one-eyed man can see; a lame man can walk; he who treads on the tail of the tiger gets bitten. Ill fortune. The braggart acts the part of a great ruler.

Interpretation: The one-eyed man can still see, the lame man can still walk, but he who over-estimates his ability to control a dangerous situation is in the position of the man who treads on the tiger's tail; he encounters disaster.

Nine in the fourth place: He treads on the tail of a tiger, but does it apprehensively and with great caution. In the end there will be good fortune.
Interpretation: Great caution is required of him who deliberately treads on a tiger's tail; an equal degree of care is necessary in taking the dangerous step that lies ahead. But such calculated bravery is justified at this time; the outcome will be fortunate.

Nine in the fifth place: He treads resolutely. Though he be firm and correct, there will be evil.
Interpretation: Although he proceeds with proper care, in the best possible manner, peril lies ahead. Great discretion is needed if disaster is to be avoided.

Nine in the sixth place: Look at the course which is being trodden and examine the omens it displays. If it be completed without failure there will be great good fortune.
Interpretation: Treading carefully as he moves forward, examining the ground for useful portents all the way, will lead him to a fortunate outcome.

Hexagram 11

T'AI

PEACE

The trigrams: K'UN: Earth, responsive. CH'IEN: Heaven, active.

THE DECISION

Peace. The small departs and the great approaches. There will be great good fortune, progress, and success.

COMMENTARY

This hexagram shows us Heaven and Earth in close communion with one another. In consequence all things, high and low, superior and inferior, intermingle and become possessed of a single aim. The lower trigram is made up of the strong and unbroken lines (Ch'ien), and the upper trigram of the weak and broken lines (K'un). The lower is the symbol of strength, and the upper the symbol of docility; the lower represents the superior man, and the upper the small man.

Thus the superior man is seen to be increasing, while the small man decreases in influence.

THE IMAGE

Heaven and Earth are in communion. The sovereign, in harmony with this, fashions and completes the courses of Heaven and Earth; he furthers the application of their fruits for the benefit of the people.

Nine in the first place: When grass is pulled up it brings with it other stalks that are attached to it. Advancing will be fortunate.
Interpretation: This indicates a fortunate time for moving ahead. One can count on the loyalty of like-minded colleagues when planning an advance.

Nine in the second place: He is tolerant when dealing with the uncultured, confidently crosses the river without a boat, does not forget what is distant, has no selfish friendships. Thus he acts in accordance with the middle way.
Interpretation: Prevailing conditions are so auspicious that he can effortlessly act in the correct manner at all times.

Nine in the third place: There is no level plain which is not succeeded by a slope; there is no peace which is not open to disturbance; there is no departure that is not followed by a return. Yet when one is firm and correct in his actions, aware of what may come, he will commit no error. There is no occasion for sadness at the prospect of certain change; by reconciling oneself to it the happiness of the present may be long enjoyed.
Interpretation: The phenomena of change should not give rise to sadness; remembering that perseverance during difficult times will see the turning of distress into good fortune. He who can rise above the vicissitudes of life will not go unrewarded.

Six in the fourth place: Ignoring his riches he unaffectedly calls on his neighbours in a trusting and sincere fashion.
Interpretation: In times of mutual trust people of all ranks intermingle in a simple and sincere manner.

Six in the fifth place: The Emperor gives his daughter in marriage to one lower than she in rank, decreeing that she must obey her husband. Happiness and great good fortune result.

Interpretation: The happy outcome follows from correct behaviour being shown during an emotionally charged situation.

Six in the sixth place: The city wall has fallen into the moat. This is not the time to go to war, but to present the situation clearly to the townspeople. Advancing in a forceful manner will lead to regret.
Interpretation: The approaching adversary cannot be averted; endeavouring to combat the evil from one's present weakened position will be of no avail. The best course would be to solicit the loyal support of one's associates, then submit to what must come to pass.

Hexagram 12

P'I

STAGNATION

The trigrams: CH'IEN: Heaven, active. K'UN: Earth, responsive.

THE DECISION

Stagnation. There is a lack of understanding between men. Such a condition is unfavourable to the superior man. The great are gone and the small approach.

COMMENTARY

Stagnation springs from the fact that Heaven and Earth are not in communion with each other, and that in consequence all things do not intermingle. The high and the low, superiors and inferiors, do not communicate with one another, and there are no well-governed states to be seen anywhere.

The lower trigram is made up of weak and broken lines, and the upper trigram of strong and undivided lines. The lower trigram is the symbol of weakness and represents the small man; the upper trigram is the symbol of strength and represents the superior man. Therefore the small man can be seen to be increasing, while the power of the superior man decreases.

THE IMAGE

Heaven and earth are not in communion. The superior man hides his virtue and avoids the calamities which threaten him. He does not allow wealth to be conferred upon him.

Progressive influences having completed their work, the processes of growth are at an end. Increasing conditions of decay must now be looked for.

THE LINES

Six in the first place: When grass is uprooted, it brings with it other stalks with which it is entwined beneath the surface of the earth. With firm correctness there will be good fortune and success.
Interpretation: When the superior man is forced by adverse circumstances to abandon his position, he takes with him like-minded men who are upright and loyal.

Six in the second place: He is patient and obedient to the demands of the time. To the small man will come good fortune, while the great man will have success.
Interpretation: Conditions favour small men: as long as they remain small. But of the superior man, greater things are required. He must meet the challenge before him with patience and fortitude, standing apart from the common crowd.

Six in the third place: He hides his shame.
Interpretation: He feels justly ashamed of his unworthy actions and tries to conceal them.

Nine in the fourth place: He acts in accordance with the ordinance of Heaven, committing no error. His companions will come and share in his happiness.
Interpretation: Carrying out the instructions issued by higher authority will bring good fortune and praise. Colleagues, too, will share in this approval.

Nine in the fifth place: The great man brings distress and obstruction to an end. But he must still exclaim 'We may perish! We may perish!' In this way the situation will become stable and firm, like a bound clump of mulberry bushes.

Interpretation: The great man is in a position to bring prevailing adversities to an end, but he needs to remain vigilant during the transition period that lies between instability and safety. He must bind all together in a progressive movement, in the way that mulberry trees are bound in order to strengthen them.

Nine in the sixth place: Stagnation is overthrown and removed. Stagnation before, happiness hereafter.

Interpretation: Stagnation is about to be overcome, giving way to joy and progress. This is inevitable; every condition eventually gives way to its opposite.

Hexagram 13

T'UNG JÊN

FELLOWSHIP

The trigrams: CH'IEN: Heaven, active. LI: Fire, clinging.

THE DECISION

Fellowship. Such union between men we find in the remote districts of the country. Progress and success are indicated. It will be advantageous to cross the great water, and to maintain a perseverance like that of the superior man.

COMMENTARY

Here the weak (second line) is in a position of influence, and responds to the strong (fifth line). Hence the title *Fellowship*.

Fellowship is brought about by the power of Heaven. The strong fifth line represents the superior man; only he can understand and influence the minds of all under Heaven.

Fellowship such as we find in remote country districts favours progress and success. Adoption of the unselfish ideals of the superior man will lead to success.

Fellowship must be based entirely on public considerations, without taint of selfishness, if it is to succeed. Such fellowship can be observed in remote districts of the country, where people are unsophisticated and free from the depraving effects of large societies. Such fellowship can cope with the greatest difficulties.

THE IMAGE

The active (Ch'ien) and the clinging (Li) come together in
fellowship. The superior man distinguishes things according to
their several kinds and classes.

THE LINES

Nine in the first place: Fellowship issuing from the gate. There
will be no error.
Interpretation: Friendly overtures will be made in an open-
handed fashion. No harm can come from accepting them.

Six in the second place: Fellowship with his kindred. There
will be occasion for regret.
Interpretation: Because of certain personal loyalties, general
fellowship is restrained and limited. This will give rise to
occasion for regret.

Nine in the third place: He hides his weapons in the thick grass
near a high vantage point. But for three years he makes no
attack.
Interpretation: Like one who delays for three years, unable to
make the decision to attack his enemies, hesitation at this point
will lead to regret. He should either take courage and attack, or
abandon the plan and go home.

Nine in the fourth place: He scales the city wall, but refrains
from attacking. There will be good fortune.
Interpretation: Viewing the enemy from the safety of his forti-
fied wall, he realizes he is not equipped to make a successful
attack. Calm appraisal of the situation at such a time will lead
to good fortune. A truce is likely.

Nine in the fifth place: The fellows weep and cry out, then
laugh. Their great army conquers, and they are brought together.

He hides his weapons in the thick grass near a high vantage point

Interpretation: After much opposition and distress victory is achieved. Opposing factions are brought together in fellowship and laughter is heard.

Nine in the sixth place: Fellowship with those in the near countryside. There will be no need for repentance.
Interpretation: Fellowship can only be achieved at this time among those close at hand. Universal fellowship is still far off, but what has already been attained gives no cause for regret.

Hexagram 14

TA YU

WEALTH

The trigrams: LI: Fire, clinging. CH'IEN: Heaven, active.

THE DECISION

Wealth. Great progress and success.

COMMENTARY

Here the weak line holds the place of honour, is supremely central, and the strong lines above and below it respond to it. Hence comes its title, Wealth.

Its attributes are strength and creativity, elegance and brightness. It responds to Heaven, and as a result all its actions occur at the proper times. Therefore it indicates great progress and success.

Prosperity and abundance and the opulence it leads to can result in dangerous pride. But here success will be accompanied by humility and discipline; no fault will be incurred.

THE IMAGE

Fire (Li) across Heaven (Ch'ien). The superior man represses what is evil and gives distinction to what is good, acting in sympathy with his Heavenly virtue.

THE LINES

Nine in the first place: He does not approach that which is harmful, and so avoids error. If he remains aware of the difficulty before him he will be blameless till the end.

Interpretation: No risks should be taken when danger threatens. If this state of affairs can be maintained no mishap can occur.

Nine in the second place: A large wagon with its load. In whatever direction progress is made, there will be no error.
Interpretation: Like he who possesses a large wagon loaded with goods, he need not fear insolvency. If, as in the case of the wagon, his strength and usefulness is channelled into a worthy cause, success will undoubtedly follow.

Nine in the third place: A prince presents his offering to the Son of Heaven. A small man would be unequal to such a duty.
Interpretation: It is in order for a great prince to offer the benefits of his wealth in the service of the Emperor; such a gesture would be above the means of a lesser man. One should be sure of one's stature before embarking on a project of great magnitude.

Nine in the fourth place: He keeps his great resources under restraint. There will be no error.
Interpretation: A major error can be avoided by restraining the impulse to use one's wealth as a lever to gain power over others. Great self-discipline is required.

Six in the fifth place: Behaviour as sincere as his own is displayed by those around him. If he displays an appropriate dignity there will be good fortune.
Interpretation: If his benevolence is not accompanied by sufficient dignity, those beneath him will withdraw the respect they have accorded him. A correct balance between benevolence and severity must be kept if good fortune is to continue for any time.

Nine in the sixth place: Heaven extends its help to him. There will be good fortune and advantage in every respect.
Interpretation: An augury of great success! Even Heaven will bestow its favour. Only a disciplined control of wealth can bring about this state of affairs.

Hexagram 15

MODESTY

The trigrams: K'UN: Earth, responsive. KÊN: Mountain, immovable.

THE DECISION

Modesty. Progress and success. The superior man, though strong, cultivates humility and thus attains continuing good fortune.

COMMENTARY

It is the way of Heaven to send its influences below, where they shine brilliantly. It is the way of Earth, being low, to raise its influences before acting.

It is the way of Heaven to diminish the full and enlarge the modest. It is the way of Earth to overthrow the full and replenish the modest. The gods bring down disaster on the full and bless the modest. It is the way of man to hate the full and love the modest. Humility displayed in a position of honour increases the radiance of that honour; displayed in a lowly position, men will not seek to brush it aside. Therefore the superior man encounters good fortune in all his undertakings.

THE IMAGE

A mountain (Kên) in the midst of the earth (K'un). The superior man diminishes what is excessive and increases what is lacking, and thus brings about a balanced equality; both within himself and in those around him.

THE LINES

Six in the first place: The superior man adds modesty to the modesty which is already within him. He may cross the great water, and there will be good fortune.

Interpretation: First restraining his ambition and achieving an attitude of true humility, he is able to successfully launch a great adventure.

Six in the second place: Modesty reveals itself. With firm correctness there will be good fortune.

Interpretation: True humility reveals itself, like the unaffected crowing of a cock, in a person's worldly acts. Such inner decorum brings about the conditions for permanent success.

Nine in the third place: The superior man, his virtue known, maintains his success to the end and enjoys good fortune.

Interpretation: The obvious merits of the superior man draw people to him; they work hard in his service and success follows naturally.

Six in the fourth place: Every intended action will benefit if modesty is displayed during its execution.

Interpretation: Ultimate success cannot be denied to one who is truly modest. By being appreciative of the work of those around him he gains their approval and their confidence.

Six in the fifth place: He gives employment to his neighbours without displaying his wealth ostentatiously. This is a favourable time to apply force where it is needed. All his actions will be favourable.

Interpretation: Although rich, the superior man's modest bearing enables him to deal with his neighbours in a relaxed fashion. Because he does not arouse antagonism in those around him, he gains approval even when he asserts his power.

Six in the sixth place: His humility is recognized. It is a favourable time for sending forth the army, but only to subdue his own towns and countryside.

Interpretation: His essential goodness and lack of personal vanity being generally recognized, the superior man is able to impose his plans for improvement on those who are beneath him, confident in the knowledge that he will not be resisted or his motives be questioned. His self-discipline will prevent him from over-reaching himself.

Hexagram 16

YÜ

CALM CONFIDENCE

The trigrams: CHÊN: Thunder, arousing. K'UN: Earth, responsive.

THE DECISION

Calm confidence. Princes may be appointed and the army sent forth with advantage.

COMMENTARY

Here the strong line gains the response of all the others, and everything willed can be carried out. This inspires calm confidence.

Such confidence results in action which is in accord with the way of Heaven and earth; therefore it favours the setting up of princes and the sending forth of armies. Because of the state of calm confidence which exists between Heaven and earth, the sun and moon do not stray from their orbits and the four seasons do not deviate from their appointed order.

The sages obey this law and therefore their punishments are just and the people willingly submit. Great indeed is the time indicated by this hexagram!

During conditions of general harmony and contentment, important appointments are rightly made and far-reaching innovations are begun. The chief minister is in the ruler's confidence and all beneath him give him respect and proper obedience.

THE IMAGE

Thunder (Chên) issues crashingly from the earth (K'un). The kings of ancient times made music and did honour to virtue, offering their praise lavishly to the Supreme One as they officiated at the sacrifices to their ancestors.

THE LINES

Six in the first place: He proclaims his pleasure and satisfaction. There will be evil.
Interpretation: Happiness reigns, but self-satisfaction and boasting will ensure that it does not endure for long.

Six in the second place: He is firm as a rock. He knows the outcome without waiting till it has come to pass. With his determination there will be good fortune.
Interpretation: Quietly and firmly following his correct course in a far-sighted manner, good fortune is assured him.

Six in the third place: He gazes upwards while indulging in feelings of pleasure and satisfaction. If only he would understand! If he delays, he will have occasion to repent.
Interpretation: Looking upwards for favours from above while at the same time remaining inactive and complacent will bring regret; only a swift understanding of his peril can avert disgrace.

Nine in the fourth place: He radiates calm confidence and thereby achieves great success. If he dispels all his doubts, friends will gather round.
Interpretation: Harmony and satisfaction approach. By maintaining his self-confidence and subduing doubts and suspicions, friends will gather round and success be assured.

Six in the fifth place: Chronically ill, he lives on without dying.
Interpretation: Illness is forecast, but it will not result in death.

His immediate position is perilous, but ultimate triumph is shown.

Six in the sixth place: Unthinkingly he devotes himself to immediate pleasure and satisfaction. But if he changes his course even after completion there will be no error.
Interpretation: Completely involved in ephemeral pleasures, he drifts towards disaster. But even at this late hour prompt action can save him.

Hexagram 17

FOLLOWING

The trigrams: TUI: Lake, joyful. CHÊN: Thunder, arousing.

THE DECISION

Following. Great progress and success. Firm correctness will be
of advantage. There will be no error.

COMMENTARY

Here the strong comes and places itself beneath the weak; we
see in the trigrams the attributes of arousal and joy. This gives
the idea of following.

Great progress, firm correctness, and no error: all under
heaven will be found following at such a time. Great indeed is
the time signified by this hexagram.

The ability to be flexible and to adapt to varying conditions
will result in success. He who is guided by his inner sense of
what is proper, who can follow as well as lead when circumstances warrant it, will attain good fortune.

When conditions are harmonious men are sure to follow, but
they will not follow one in whom they have no trust.

THE IMAGE

Thunder (Chên) in the midst of a lake (Tui). The superior man,
when it is getting dark, enters his house and rests.

Nine in the first place: He changes the object of his attentions. If he be firm and correct good fortune will follow. Going outside his door and meeting people will bring him merit.

Interpretation: A change of pursuit is indicated. This must be inspired from within, after which firm resolution will bring it to a successful conclusion. The following of a new path will lead to successful relationships.

Six in the second place: He chooses the little boy and rejects the man of age and experience.

Interpretation: He is in danger of choosing his associates unwisely.

Six in the third place: He chooses the man of experience and releases the little boy. By doing this he will get what he seeks. It will be of advantage to keep always to what is firm and correct.

Interpretation: Such a wise decision will lead to the fulfilment of his hopes, but caution is required when following through this design.

Nine in the fourth place: He gains followers. Though he be firm and correct, there will be evil. But if he acts in all sincerity, what error can he fall into?

Interpretation: Danger comes from the self-seeking behaviour of followers. Though the leader stands above such actions, he may unwittingly be associated with them. Only by showing his personal integrity in a clear and unmistakable fashion can this be avoided.

Nine in the fifth place: Sincerely he follows all that is excellent. There will be good fortune.

Interpretation: The sincerity of the ruler is reflected in the trust of his followers.

Six in the sixth place: Because of his sincerity his followers cling to him as if bound fast. The king presents his sacrifice on the western mountain.

Interpretation: Following what is right with deepest sincerity attracts the faith of the people, therefore the king makes offerings on the western mountain. By following the right way with firmness one becomes a leader. But this may involve supplanting one's previous superior.

Hexagram 18

DECAY

The trigrams: KÊN: Mountain, immovable. SUN: Wind, gentle.

THE DECISION

Decay. Progress and success. There will be advantage in crossing the great water. But he should consider for three days before commencing, and for three days after commencing.

COMMENTARY

Here we have the strong above and the weak below; the gentle is combined with the immovable. This indicates great success. There will be good order in everything under Heaven. He who presses forward will encounter important business which must be done. The ending of confusion signals the beginning of order; such is the way of Heaven.

Success in arresting decay and restoring soundness is indicated, but great efforts such as that entailed in crossing the great water are necessary. Careful appraisal of the situation is needed before action can safely be taken, and vigilance is required afterwards to avoid a repetition of the trouble.

THE IMAGE

Wind (Sun) below the mountain (Kên). The superior man inspires the people and gives strength to their virtue.

Six in the first place: The son deals with the troubles caused by his father. If he is competent the father will escape all blame. There is peril, but good fortune will appear in the end.
Interpretation: The state of decay, though advanced, is not yet past repair. Adequate work can restore what has been lost.

Nine in the second place: The son deals with the troubles caused by his mother. He should not pursue his course too diligently.
Interpretation: A son should proceed in a gentle manner when rectifying the mistakes caused by his mother. Decay caused by another's weakness can only be restored slowly and by proceeding with great sensitivity.

Nine in the third place: The son deals with the troubles caused by his father. There may be some small occasion for regret, but no great error.
Interpretation: Dealing with the troubles caused by his father, the son may proceed too energetically; but in this instance too great an effort is better than too little. Minor losses may be incurred, but nothing outstanding.

Six in the fourth place: Complacently he observes the troubles caused by his father. If he continues in this manner he will have cause for regret.
Interpretation: Indulgent tolerance of conditions of decay will involve one in grave difficulties at a later date.

Six in the fifth place: He deals with the troubles caused by his father. He will be praised for his efforts.
Interpretation: Because he deals voluntarily with the decay caused by those who have gone before, he receives approval and the praise due to him.

Nine in the sixth place: He does not serve either king or lord, but in a lofty spirit he attends to his own affairs.
Interpretation: Uncorrupted, he proceeds along his own path. Because his motives are pure he can do this without falling into error.

Hexagram 19

LIN

GETTING AHEAD

The trigrams: K'UN: Earth, responsive. TUI: Lake, joyful.

THE DECISION

Getting ahead. There will be great progress and success. Firm correctness will be of advantage. In the eighth month there will be evil.

COMMENTARY

Here the strong lines are gradually increasing and advancing. The lower trigram signifies pleasure, and the upper compliance. A strong line occupies the centre of the lower trigram, and other lines respond to it. Great progress combined with correctness reveals the way of Heaven, but the advancing power will lose its impetus after a time.

Authority approaches: to inspect, to comfort, and to rule. Such action will be powerful and successful, but it must be borne in mind that everything is subject to change and that progress will eventually give way to decay. This must always be taken into account when plans are made.

THE IMAGE

The earth (K'un) rises above the waters of the lake (Tui). The superior man is inexhaustible in his teachings, nourishing and supporting the people endlessly.

Nine in the first place: He advances in the company of another. His firm correctness will bring him good fortune.

Interpretation: Advancing in company, his strength must be tempered with caution and the use of correct aids to progress.

Nine in the second place: He advances in company. There will be good fortune. Such progress will be advantageous in every way.

Interpretation: His associates approve of his policies and they advance as one. The outcome of their solidarity will be highly favourable.

Six in the third place: He is happy to advance, but no direction offers him advantage. If he shows anxiety there will be no error.

Interpretation: An impulse to make progress, if given way to, will not be fortunate in its outcome. If he takes note of his misgivings and remains where he is, mistakes can be avoided.

Six in the fourth place: He advances in great style. There will be no error.

Interpretation: He makes progress in the best possible manner, keeping always to the correct path.

Six in the fifth place: He advances wisely, as befits a great ruler. There will be good fortune.

Interpretation: Wise authority advances its interests by employing competent executives.

Six in the sixth place: He advances in an honest and generous manner. There will be good fortune and no error.

Interpretation: Straightforward generosity furthers an advance. There will be good fortune and an avoidance of mistakes.

Hexagram 20

KUAN

CONTEMPLATION

The trigrams: SUN: Wind, gentle. K'UN: Earth, responsive.

THE DECISION

Contemplation. The ritual washing of hands has taken place, but the sacrifice has not yet been made. Sincerity and a dignified bearing command respect.

COMMENTARY

This hexagram is made up of the trigrams representing docility and flexibility, and the ruling line is situated in the centre of the upper trigram. From its high position it contemplates everything that occurs in the world beneath.

When he acts with sincerity and an appearance of dignity, all beneath look up to him and are transformed. They contemplate the way of Heaven and observe how the seasons follow their cycle without error. The sages, in accordance with this same way, gave their instructions and all under Heaven submit to them.

The superior man contemplates the law of the universe and the recurring cycle of the seasons. Acting as a vehicle for the power of Heaven, he achieves greatness.

THE IMAGE

The wind (Sun) moves across the face of the earth (K'un). The ancient kings visited the different regions of the kingdom, observing the ways of the people and issuing their instructions.

Six in the first place: He looks at things in the manner of a boy. This is not a matter for blame in men of inferior rank, but is regrettable in superior men.
Interpretation: Childish immaturity is acceptable in lesser men, but not in one who is great.

Six in the second place: He peeps out from a door. Such behaviour would be advantageous in a woman.
Interpretation: Observing things as if one were peering round the edge of a door is acceptable behaviour in a woman, being in accord with the female character, but such a restricted viewpoint is shameful in one who holds an important position in the world.

Six in the third place: He contemplates the course of his own life, deciding whether to advance or retreat.
Interpretation: By studying the course of one's life one is able to judge when it is safe to advance, and when it is prudent to retreat.

Six in the fourth place: He contemplates the glory of the kingdom. It will further him to become a guest of the king.
Interpretation: By observing the state of the realm he is able to gauge whether or not it would be to his advantage to ally himself with it. He should study the situation carefully before committing himself.

Nine in the fifth place: He contemplates the course of his life. Being a superior man, he will thus avoid falling into error.
Interpretation: The superior man avoids mistakes by studying his own life and the lives of those beneath him.

Nine in the sixth place: He contemplates his own character to see whether or not he is indeed a superior man. He will not fall into error.
Interpretation: By examining himself in a critical manner the superior man resolves his self-doubts.

Hexagram 21

SHIH HO

BITING THROUGH

The trigrams: LI: Fire, clinging. CHÊN: Thunder, arousing.

THE DECISION

Biting through. Successful progress. It will be advantageous to use legal restraints.

COMMENTARY

Biting through signifies success. In this hexagram the strong and weak lines are equally divided. The lower trigram denotes arousal and the upper trigram brightness; thunder and lightning come together and create brilliance. The weak lines are in the centre and rise upwards. Although this process is improper, it does further the exercise of the law.

By gnawing through what restrains them the jaws are able to come together. This principle can be applied to state affairs. Remove the obstacles to political and social union, and high and low will come together with a good understanding. How are such obstacles to be overcome? By the power of the law. Such restraint is certain to be successful.

THE IMAGE

Thunder (Chên) and lightning (Li). The ancient kings devised their penalties in an intelligent manner, then put forth their code of law.

Nine in the first place: His feet are shackled, hiding his toes. There will be no error.
Interpretation: Because the evil is still in its early stages, such a mild punishment is sufficient to curb it.

Six in the second place: He bites through the soft flesh, then continues until he has bitten through the nose. There will be no error.
Interpretation: For punishment to be effective it must be carried through to the end.

Six in the third place: He chews dried meat, and is inadvertently poisoned. There will be occasion for regret, but no error.
Interpretation: Enforcing punishment in a case which is no longer relevant to the needs of the day will bring down criticism upon his head. But it is proper that justice is done.

Nine in the fourth place: Biting through meat dried on the bone, he exercises his judicial functions. He must realize the difficulty of his task and be firm. In this way there will be good fortune.
Interpretation: He must fully realize that the case before him is not easy; only by acting in a firm and just manner can he attain good fortune.

Six in the fifth place: Chewing dried meat, he finds a piece of gold in it. If he be firm and correct, and realizes the danger which lies before him, there will be no error.
Interpretation: The finding of metal in one's meat indicates unexpected setbacks ahead, but as the metal is gold this may turn out to be a blessing in disguise!

Nine in the sixth place: He wears a wooden yoke which covers his ears. There will be evil.
Interpretation: Deaf to all caution, he goes heedlessly on his way, getting farther and farther from his right path.

Hexagram 22

ADORNMENT

The trigrams: KÊN: Mountain, immovable. LI: Fire, clinging.

THE DECISION

Adornment. Success. Small undertakings are favoured.

COMMENTARY

Here the weak line ornaments the strong lines of the lower trigram, indicating success. But in the upper trigram the strong line ornaments the weak ones, indicating that the advantages to to be gained are small ones.

Brilliance regulated by the forces of stability describes the adornments of human society. We observe the ornamental patterns displayed in the Heavens and thereby ascertain the cycle of the seasons. We observe the ornamental patterns displayed in society and comprehend how the processes of change are accomplished everywhere.

Elegant adornment should form part of human society as it is a part of nature, but it must always take second place to what is of real importance. If adornment is allowed to play a dominant role in society there will be little advantage in it.

THE IMAGE

Fire (Li) under the mountain (Kên). The superior man acts in a brilliant fashion when dealing with the day-to-day process of government, but dare not do this when deciding matters of law. Sobriety is then required.

THE LINES

Nine in the first place: He adorns his feet, leaves the carriage, and proceeds on foot.
Interpretation: Confidence in the future allows him to discard the outer trappings of authority.

Six in the second place: He adorns his beard.
Interpretation: What may be classed as mere vanity takes on higher significance when it is performed as a preliminary to an important undertaking. Then it shows proper respect for the solemnity of the occasion.

Nine in the third place: Richly adorned, he gleams as if covered in fresh dew. Firm persistence will ensure his good fortune.
Interpretation: Such good fortune will be certain if he acts confidently, as if it had already arrived, while at the same time remaining alert and diligent in his efforts.

Six in the fourth place: He is adorned all in white, and mounted on a winged white horse he is in pursuit; not as a robber, but as a suitor.
Interpretation: His motives, though completely honourable, may come under suspicion. Something more solid than promises and a fine appearance is needed to win the day.

Six in the fifth place: Elegantly he strolls through the heights and gardens, but the roll of silk he bears as a gift is small and coarse in texture. Humiliation lies ahead if he is thought to be miserly, but in the end good fortune will prevail.
Interpretation: The hollowness of his pretensions is about to be revealed, but the ensuing disgrace will be temporary.

He is adorned all in white, and mounted on a winged white horse
he is in pursuit; not as a robber, but as a suitor

Nine in the sixth place: Simple white adornment. There will be no error.
Interpretation: By reducing his plan to true simplicity he will ensure its acceptance. Solid worth is better than surface attractiveness.

Hexagram 23

PO

SHEDDING

The trigrams: KÊN: Mountain, immovable. K'UN: Earth, responsive.

THE DECISION

Shedding. It would not be advantageous to make a move in any direction.

COMMENTARY

Here the weak lines are about to transform the strong line into one of themselves. Small men are now multiplying and increasing their influence. The superior man notes the appearance of conditions symbolized by this hexagram, and stops trying to advance. He appreciates the cycles of decrease and increase, of completion and decadence, as revealed by the heavenly bodies.

Small men have gradually replaced good men until but one remains. The forces operating against him are too great for him to prevail against them. But the fashion of political life passes away; if he waits, a change for the better will shortly develop.

THE IMAGE

The mountain (Kên) rises above the earth (K'un). Those in a superior position seek to strengthen the ones beneath them. In this way they secure their own peace and stability.

Six in the first place: The legs of the bed are being sawn through. All rectitude is about to be destroyed. There will be evil.
Interpretation: His position is being undermined. Like the occupant of a bed when its legs are being sawn through, all he can do is wait for the painful outcome.

Six in the second place: The frame of the bed is being broken. Moral uprightness is about to be destroyed, and there will be evil.
Interpretation: Disaster approaches and his personal integrity is at stake.

Six in the third place: He helps to overturn the bed. There will be no error.
Interpretation: By using his strength and superior virtue to aid the tide of events, he avoids being destroyed by it.

Six in the fourth place: The bed is overturned and its occupant is exposed to his enemies. There will be evil.
Interpretation: Danger approaches and he is helpless.

Six in the fifth place: He leads his subjects like a string of fishes, obtaining for them the favour of the king. Every advantage will follow and no blame will be incurred.
Interpretation: Small men willingly submit to the authority of one above them who has their best interests at heart. He who takes the responsibility for leading others need not fear the outcome of his actions.

Nine in the sixth place: He is like a great fruit which has not been eaten. He goes before the people as if riding in a triumphal chariot, while lesser men ruin themselves.
Interpretation: He will survive and remain undamaged by his present adversity. Public support will reinforce his ambitions and his opponents will be successfully overthrown.

Hexagram 24

RETURNING

The trigrams: K'UN: Earth, responsive. CHÊN: Thunder, arousing.

THE DECISION

Returning. Freedom and progress lie ahead. The superior man can come and go without being opposed, friends come to see him and after seven days return with no error having been made. Movement in any direction will be of advantage.

COMMENTARY

Here the strong line reappears at the bottom of the hexagram, intimating the return of progressive trends. The natural order now favours progress, therefore he can come and go freely. All his actions are in harmony with the will of Heaven, and he can now advance successfully because the strong lines are advancing.

Do we not see here the moving intelligence of Heaven and Earth? Change is the law of nature and of society; when decay has reached its climax a recovery must take place. Brightness will increase day by day and month by month.

THE IMAGE

Thunder (Chên) from within the earth (K'un). The ancient kings closed the passes between states on the day of the winter Solstice. Travelling merchants could not then pursue their journeys and princes could not carry out the customary inspection of their states.

Nine in the first place: He returns to his true path after a minor diversion. He will have no cause for regret and great good fortune will come to him.
Interpretation: Self-discipline is required until the danger is over.

Six in the second place: He makes an admirable return. There will be good forutne.
Interpretation: This is achieved through the benevolence of a good man.

Six in the third place: He goes and returns again and again. Though the position is dangerous there will be no error.
Interpretation: Evil may be prevented by a realization of danger allied to great caution.

Six in the fourth place: He sets out in the company of others but returns alone.
Interpretation: This is auspicious because the solitary path is the right one for him at this time.

Six in the fifth place: He returns in a noble and upright manner. There will be no ground for repentance.
Interpretation: An awareness of his failings and the desire to rectify them will keep him from disgrace.

Six in the sixth place: He returns in a disordered manner. There will be evil, errors, and even calamities. If his efforts result in the sending forth of the army the outcome will be a great defeat. Even the ruler will be involved, and ten years will not be sufficient time in which to repair the disaster.
Interpretation: He returns at a time when all movement is inauspicious, and his mistaken views will lead to general danger and instability. If his opinions prevail those associated with him will suffer a great defeat. Such a disaster cannot be rectified easily, not even in ten years!

Hexagram 25

WU WANG

SIMPLE INTEGRITY

The trigrams: CH'IEN: Heaven, active. CHÊN: Thunder, arousing.

THE DECISION

Simple integrity. Great progress and success. There will be advantage in being firm. If he does not act correctly he will fall into error and it will not further him to move in any direction.

COMMENTARY

Here the strong first line descends from the upper trigram and becomes lord of the lower trigram, joining movement to strength. The strong fifth line is responded to by the weak second line, indicating progress which proceeds from firm adherence to the law of Heaven.

He who does not act in the correct manner will fall into error and nothing will further his aims. How can he who acts thus, yet believes himself free from error, hope to progress? Can anything be done advantageously by him who does not accord with the will of Heaven?

If his actions are not carried out with integrity he will commit serious mistakes, in which case no subsequent move can repair the error. The nearer he approaches the ideal of simple integrity the more powerful will be his influence, the greater his success. The quality of simple integrity is characteristic of

Heaven and of the highest type of humanity. The superior man never swerves from being correct.

THE IMAGE

Thunder (Chên) rolls beneath the sky (Ch'ien). To everything is attributed its true nature, free from insincerity. The ancient kings, in complete accordance with the seasons, nourished all things.

THE LINES

Nine in the first place: He is free from all insincerity, and his progress will be accompanied by good fortune.
Interpretation: By clinging to his integrity all his actions will be favourable.

Six in the second place: He reaps without having ploughed, he gathers the third year's crop from his fields without having cultivated during the first year. Such is his virtue that there will be advantage in everything he attempts.
Interpretation: Entirely free from selfish motives, he treads the path of virtue for its own sake. Therefore all his activities will be successful.

Six in the third place: Calamity happens even to him who is free from all insincerity. A tethered ox is stolen by a passer-by and the farmer's neighbours are blamed for the theft.
Interpretation: He must remain aware of the possibility of evil even while acting with integrity himself.

Nine in the fourth place: If he can remain firm and correct, there will be no error.
Interpretation: Firm persistence and the courage to trust his own virtue is needed at such a time.

Nine in the fifth place: Although he has integrity, yet he falls ill. Let him not use medicine and he will have occasion for joy.

Interpretation: He need not be anxious; without effort his safe path through current difficulties will be revealed.

Nine in the sixth place: Although free from all insincerity, yet he is sure to fall into error if he attempts to advance.

Interpretation: Movement of any kind will not be advantageous. At such times one should rest and remain secure in one's present position.

Hexagram 26

TA CH'U

ACCUMULATION THROUGH RESTRAINT

The trigrams: KÊN: Mountain, immovable. CH'IEN: Heaven, active.

THE DECISION

Accumulation through restraint. It will be advantageous to be firm and correct. If he does not reserve his talents for the benefit of his immediate circle, but places himself at the service of the king, there will be good fortune. It will further him to cross the great water.

COMMENTARY

Here we have the attributes of great strength and firmness, which shed a brilliant radiance round about and renew virtue daily. The strong line occupies the highest place, suggesting the value of talent and virtue. The upper trigram contains power sufficient to restrain the strongest, pointing to the benefits of firm correctness. Good fortune is forecast for him who does not seek to keep his wealth within his own circle, but who benefits all men. To cross the great water at this time would find favour with the will of Heaven.

Engaging in the public service, enjoying the favour of the king, he may undertake the most difficult enterprises.

THE IMAGE

Heaven (Ch'ien) in the midst of a mountain (Kên). The superior man stores in his memory the words and deeds of men of ancient times, thus adding to his virtue.

THE LINES

Nine in the first place: He occupies a dangerous position. It would be wise for him to advance no further.
Interpretation: Great restraint is called for.

Nine in the second place: The restraining strap beneath the carriage has been removed.
Interpretation: The danger increases. Advancing further would place him in grave peril.

Nine in the third place: He advances rapidly, pulled by strong horses. If he realizes the difficulties that lie before him, prepares himself and acts with foresight, he will attain success.
Interpretation: But cautious restraint is still very necessary.

Six in the fourth place: The young bull wears a headboard. There will be good fortune.
Interpretation: Precautionary restraint is advised right from the beginning, even before any need for it is shown; as in the case of one who places a wooden guard over the undeveloped horns of a young bull.

Six in the fifth place: The tusks of a gelded boar. There will be good fortune.
Interpretation: If a powerful boar is gelded, he has little inclination to use his tusks. By restraining evil at its source its power is neutralized and good can prevail.

Nine in the sixth place: He commands the way of Heaven. There will be great progress.
Interpretation: The time for necessary restraint is over; due to his accumulated virtue he is as if in command of Heaven itself. His advance cannot fail.

Hexagram 27

I

NOURISHMENT

The trigrams: KÊN: Mountain, immovable. CHEN: Thunder, arousing.

THE DECISION

Nourishment. With firm correctness there will be good fortune. Pay heed to the manner in which people nourish others, and watch what they seek out for their own nourishment.

COMMENTARY

When nourishment is of the right sort, firm persistence will lead to good fortune. We must look at those we wish to nourish as well as seeing to our own nourishment. Heaven and earth nourish all things, and the sages nourish talented and virtuous men that they might offer sustenance to all the world. Great is the effect of timely nourishment!

The superior man nourishes his body and his mind, his own self and that of others. The kind and degree of nourishment to be applied is decided by him in the light of his own virtue. Nourishment must be both harmonious and correct if it is to succeed in its aim.

THE IMAGE

Thunder (Chên) at the foot of the mountain (Kên). The superior man keeps a careful watch on his words and regulates his eating and drinking.

Nine in the first place: You release your magic tortoise and look at me till your lower jaw hangs down. There will be evil.
Interpretation: Although able to nourish himself without hardship, like the sacred tortoise which lives on air, he stares in envy at another with his mouth hanging open. No good can come of this.

Six in the second place: He looks downward for nourishment in an improper manner, or else seeks it in the heights above. If he persists there will be evil.
Interpretation: He seeks nourishment below and above, neglecting his proper place. Progress in either direction will be unfavourable.

Six in the third place: He wilfully refrains from taking nourishment. However he acts there will be evil. For a space of ten years any action he undertakes will not lead to any advantage for him.
Interpretation: He who considers himself completely self-sufficient, rejecting all fruitful contacts, depletes his store of virtue.

Six in the fourth place: He looks down, seeking to give nourishment. He glares with the unwavering look of a tiger as he examines those below. There is no error.
Interpretation: Because his concern is for the welfare of others, not the advancement of himself, his actions are without blame.

Six in the fifth place: He acts contrary to what is normal and proper, but if he remains firm there will be good fortune. He should not at this time try to cross the great water.
Interpretation: He is not equal to the demands of his high position, but if he is able to rely on a wise superior for advice good fortune may still be his. But he must not attempt major undertakings.

He looks down, seeking to give nourishment. He glares with the unwavering look of a tiger as he examines those below

Nine in the sixth place: He is the source of nourishment. Though his position is perilous, there will be good fortune. It will be to his advantage to cross the great water.

Interpretation: He is the great teacher, the dispenser of nourishment to all under Heaven. His task is hard and his responsibility great, but being aware of these things he proves himself equal to them.

Hexagram 28

TA KUO

EXCESS

The trigrams: TUI: Lake, joyful. SUN: Wind, gentle.

THE DECISION

Excess. The roof-beam is strained to breaking point. Movement of any kind will be favourable. There will be success.

COMMENTARY

Here the combined power of the strong lines is altogether too excessive. Both the bottom and top lines are weak, and the hexagram as a whole suggests an overloaded roof-beam. However, strong lines occupy the central positions of both trigrams, revealing that success may yet be attained. Great indeed is the work to be carried out at this crucial time.

When the main roof-beam of a house bears too great a weight, collapse is imminent. This extreme situation cannot last, but disaster can be avoided by speedy action.

Extraordinary times require that one of exceptional gifts be entrusted with the conduct of affairs. Understanding of the danger caused by excess, followed by swift and sensitive action to avert it, will have a fortunate outcome.

THE IMAGE

Trees (Sun) hidden beneath the waters of the lake (Tui). The superior man stands alone and has no fear. He retires from the world with no regret.

Six in the first place: He places mats made of white rushes beneath things spread on the ground. There will be no error.
Interpretation: White rushes are rare, and their use as mats shows that he is taking pains to impress. Such meticulous attention to details will lead to success.

Nine in the second place: A decayed willow tree puts forth new shoots; an old husband possesses a young wife. There will be advantage on every side.
Interpretation: As an old man can yet produce children by his young wife, so can approaching failure be turned into success by embracing new ideas.

Nine in the third place: The main roof-beam sags dangerously. Misfortune will follow.
Interpretation: Taking on too great a burden against the advice of his colleagues will entail the loss of their support and subsequent failure.

Nine in the fourth place: The main roof-beam is supported. There will be good fortune. But reliance on weak helpers leads to misfortune.
Interpretation: Danger is averted by the support of others, but if this support is relied on to excess success will not endure.

Nine in the fifth place: The decayed willow produces only flowers, no new shoots. An old wife will produce no children. There can be neither blame nor praise.
Interpretation: Devoting one's energies to an outworn cause will not lead to success or failure, but can result only in stagnation.

Six in the sixth place: While fording the stream the water rises over his head. There will be misfortune but no grounds for blame.

Interpretation: While undertaking a correct course of action, he is overwhelmed by adverse circumstances, Herein lies misfortune, but as his motives were blameless he need not fear censure.

(Note: Each of the eight trigrams has several attributes, the most important of which are given beneath each hexagram. Other meanings sometimes occur in the text, however. The trigram SUN, in particular, can signify wood or trees, in addition to its main attributes of wind and gentle; these alternative meanings are revealed in the above hexagram, for example.)

Hexagram 29

K'AN

THE PERILOUS CHASM

The trigrams: K'AN: Water, dangerous. K'AN: Water, dangerous.

THE DECISION

The perilous chasm. Sincerity and mental alertness will encourage success. Firm action will be of advantage.

COMMENTARY

One chasm succeeds another. Water flows ever onwards; even while flowing through a dangerous chasm it keeps its true nature. He of penetrating mind, who can understand this lesson, will see the successful outcome of his efforts. This is indicated by the strong line in the centre of the lower trigram. Firm action will be of advantage: advance will be followed by achievement.

Dangers issuing from Heaven cannot be overcome, but the greatest difficulties of earth are merely mountains, rivers, hills, and cliffs. Kings and princes use such natural hazards to protect their territories. Great indeed is this lesson concerning times of peril!

Danger lies ahead, like a perilous chasm filled with rushing water. If progress is to be made despite such an obstacle, it must be encountered in an attitude of sincere honesty, with a mind which is sharp, lucid, and penetrating. These conditions being fulfilled, the outcome will be fortunate.

THE IMAGE

Water (K'an) flows on continuously. The superior man firmly maintains his inward integrity and virtuous conduct, and proceeds with his teaching of others.

THE LINES

Six in the first place: Deep in the chasm, he enters a cavern. There will be evil.
Interpretation: He is hopelessly lost, unable to find his way. No one can help him and he can by his own efforts only involve himself more deeply in danger.

Nine in the second place: He is deep within the perilous chasm. Only in small matters will he have success.
Interpretation: Unable to escape from the danger, at least he does not involve himself more deeply in it.

He is bound with thick cords and restrained by a thicket of thorns

Six in the third place: Whether he descends or ascends he remains confronted by the chasm. Peril surrounds him and he cannot rest. His best endeavours to escape can only lead him deeper into the pit. All he can do is wait.

Interpretation: He is in a highly dangerous situation. Action of any kind will be dangerous. Patience is essential.

Six in the fourth place: Simply a jar of wine, a basket of rice, and earthenware bowls. He instructs his ruler as best he may. In the end there will be no error.

Interpretation: Ostentation is not necessary in times of great peril. True simplicity can gain all that is required: Like he who prepares a simple feast, having only small quantities of wine and rice and earthenware vessels, yet who by his gesture gains the ear of his superior. No error can come from this, though results may be delayed.

Nine in the fifth place: The chasm is not yet full, but order will soon be restored. There will be no error.

Interpretation: Although the chasm is not yet filled with water, soon it will spill over and flow away. In this way danger will shortly be dispelled and order re-established.

Six in the sixth place: He is bound with thick cords and restrained by a thicket of thorns. For three years he finds no way of escape. There will be evil.

Interpretation: He is without hope of release from his predicament. All he can do is wait.

Hexagram 30

LI

BRILLIANT BEAUTY

The trigrams: LI: Fire, clinging. LI: Fire, clinging.

THE DECISION

Brilliant beauty. Perseverance in the right way brings freedom and success. Caring for cows brings good fortune.

COMMENTARY

Li signifies dependence. The sun and moon are dependent on Heaven; all the grains, grasses, and trees are dependent on the earth. The fiery brilliance produced by these two trigrams coming together in a correct manner results in the transforming and perfecting of all under the sky.

The weak second line occupies a central and proper position, intimating success.

The existence of man is dependent on many things; only by placing one's trust in the way of the universe can success be achieved. Only by total dependence on the natural order can the world be changed for the better. This is illustrated by the docility of the contented cow who, by submitting to a higher authority, finds happiness.

THE IMAGE

Brilliance (Li) repeated. The superior man encourages the brilliant beauty of his own true self to unfold, and with it he illuminates the four quarters of the world.

Nine in the first place: He is ready to move, but only with confused steps. If he walks carefully and reverently he will make no mistake.
Interpretation: The way ahead is not clear. Proceeding carefully, concentrating on the solution of each problem as it occurs, will lead to success.

Six in the second place: Yellow light. There will be great good fortune.
Interpretation: Yellow is the colour of sunlight at noon. It symbolizes the middle way, the ideal course of action that lies between two extremes. Proceeding along such a path will lead to good fortune.

Nine in the third place: In the light of the setting sun young men beat their cooking pots and sing, while old men groan and wail. There will be evil.
Interpretation: His present run of success will not continue. Neither feverish activity nor blank despair will help matters. Quiet preparation for the difficulties ahead is the best course to take.

Nine in the fourth place: Its coming is sudden. Equally quickly it dies and is lost. How abruptly it is rejected!
Interpretation: Action which is too hasty can have no lasting effect. Unexpected good fortune will not endure.

Six in the fifth place: Torrents of tears, sorrowful groans, piteous sighs. Yet there will be good fortune.
Interpretation: Prevailing conditions produce anxiety and apprehension, but this show of grief in itself proves that the right path is being followed. Good fortune lies ahead.

Nine in the sixth place: The king goes forth to chastise the rebels. He destroys the chiefs, sparing their followers. There will be no error.

Interpretation: Discipline, whether of oneself or others, is best achieved by destroying the root of the trouble. Too harsh measures defeat their own purpose. Considerate action will ensure success.

Hexagram 31

HSIEN

MUTUAL ATTRACTION

The trigrams: TUI: Lake, joyful. KÊN: Mountain, immovable.

THE DECISION

Mutual attraction. Firm correctness will lead to success. There is advantage in marrying a young girl. There will be good fortune.

COMMENTARY

Here the weak trigram is above and the strong one below. Their influences are mutually attractive and therefore they are able to come together; the immovable and the joyful are united, the male beneath the female. Therefore there will be good fortune.

Heaven and earth attract each other, and the transformation and creation of all things is the result. The sages attract the minds of men and universal harmony and peace ensue. If we look at the nature of these influences the true character of Heaven and earth and of all things can be seen.

Mutual attraction leads the man to submit himself to the weaker girl. In the same way the superior man unselfishly submits to the influences of the universe, and is rewarded by Heaven.

THE IMAGE

The lake (Tui) is sited on the mountain (Kên). The superior man keeps his mind free from all preoccupations, and is open to receive the approaches of all who come to him.

Six in the first place: He wriggles his toes.
Interpretation: However much a man may wriggle his toes it will not enable him to walk. Intentions are not enough: action must follow.

Six in the second place: He flexes the calves of his legs. Evil approaches. If he can refrain from moving there will yet be good fortune.
Interpretation: Although he is eager to advance, this is not the time for action. Patience is advised.

Nine in the third place: He moves his thighs restlessly, and is unable to resist following those he looks up to. Such lack of self-control will lead to regret.
Interpretation: Being influenced by those who are not worthy of one's respect involves one in unnecessary danger.

Nine in the fourth place: He acts with a proper firmness. Such discipline will lead to good fortune and will prevent all occasion for repentance. If he is restless and undisciplined, only his close friends will take him seriously.
Interpretation: He must beware of giving way to unhelpful outside influences. Keeping steadfastly to the right path will attract worthwhile supporters to his cause.

Nine in the fifth place: He moves the skin that covers his backbone. There will be no occasion for regret.
Interpretation: Such a movement cannot influence his actions, therefore it does not constitute a hazard in the way of his progress. This implies that purposeful movement is not advised.

Six in the sixth place: He exercises his tongue and jaws continually.
Interpretation: He does this only to try and influence others through trivial chatter and flattery. The outcome will be evil.

Hexagram 32

HÊNG

LONG DURATION

The trigrams: CHÊN: Thunder, arousing. SUN: Wind, gentle.

THE DECISION

Long duration. Successful progress and no error. Advantage will come from being firm and correct. Movement in any direction will be fortunate.

COMMENTARY

Here the strong trigram is above and the weak trigram below. Thunder and wind are united; the combination of gentleness and active arousal, in which all the lines respond to one another.

The way of Heaven and earth endures long without stopping; when the motive power is spent it will begin again. Obeying the way of Heaven, the sun and moon perpetuate their brilliance. The four seasons, by their changes and transformations, perpetuate the creation of all things. The sages persevere long in their course, and all under the sky is made perfect. When we study the causes of their long endurance, the true nature of Heaven, earth, and all things can be seen.

THE IMAGE

Thunder (Chên) and wind (Sun). The superior man stands firm and does not allow himself to be swayed.

Six in the first place: He is concerned with his own endurance. Even if he acts correctly there will be evil. No advantage can come to him.

Interpretation: Even if he perseveres greatly his misguided efforts can only result in failure. Filling the mind with thoughts of personal endurance allows no room for good fortune to enter.

Nine in the second place: All occasion for regret disappears.

Interpretation: This is because he is able to contain himself within reasonable limits.

Nine in the third place: He does not maintain his virtue in an unwavering manner, and thus lays himself open to disgrace. However firmly he may act he will have cause for regret.

Interpretation: Although he tries to follow a true path, circumstances work against him and he cannot endure.

Nine in the fourth place: There is no game in the field.

Interpretation: No amount of determined endurance on the part of the hunter will produce game if the field is empty.

Six in the fifth place: He virtuously maintains traditional marital fidelity. In a wife such virtue is fortunate; in a husband, evil.

Interpretation: A wife, being conscious of her weakness, should be docilely submissive. But a husband should assert himself and lay down the rule of what is right.

Six in the sixth place: He acts constantly in an excited manner. There will be evil.

Interpretation: His power is soon exhausted and his violent efforts can only lead to failure. Great restraint is required of him.

Hexagram 33

WITHDRAWAL

The trigrams: CH'IEN: Heaven, active. KÊN: Mountain, immovable.

THE DECISION

Withdrawal. Success. It will be advantageous to persist in small matters.

COMMENTARY

This hexagram shows that even withdrawal can have a successful outcome. A strong line occupies the fifth place, and the other lines respond to it. It acts according to the necessities of the time.

'It will be advantageous to persist in small matters' means that progressive trends are withdrawing, and only small things can flourish.

When small men multiply and increase in power, the requirements of the time cause superior men to withdraw before them. By firm correctness the threatened evil may be arrested to a small extent, but correct timing is of great importance if the withdrawal is to be orderly.

THE IMAGE

The mountain (Kên) beneath the sky (Ch'ien). The superior man keeps small men at a distance; not by exhibiting anger but by maintaining a dignified reserve.

Six in the first place: Retiring at the tail. There is peril. No progress should be made.

Interpretation: He retires to the tail-end of his company. The position is dangerous in the extreme and no movement should be attempted. Hurrying away will only aggravate the evil.

Six in the second place: He holds fast to his purpose as if bound to it by unbreakable bonds of yellow ox-hide.

Interpretation: Such strength of purpose shown when withdrawal is necessary is very commendable.

Nine in the third place: He is forced to retire as if bound: to his distress and peril. If he had dealt with those who restrain him as if they were servants and concubines, the outcome would have been more fortunate.

Interpretation: If he allowed small men less familiarity in their dealings with him he would be able to retain the upper hand in his negotiations with them. As it is, they impede his movements.

Nine in the fourth place: He withdraws, having no choice in the matter. The superior man still attains good fortune, but this is impossible for the lesser man.

Interpretation: The superior man submits, knowing that good fortune will return to him in due season. The small man cannot attain this degree of objectivity.

Nine in the fifth place: He withdraws in an admirable way. With firm correctness there will be good fortune.

Interpretation: If one can take the decision to withdraw before it is forced on one, the retreat can be carried out in a controlled manner and the foundations of future success be laid.

Nine in the sixth place: He retires in a noble way. This will be advantageous in every way.

Interpretation: He retains his vigour and happily carries out what must be done.

Hexagram 34

VIGOROUS STRENGTH

The trigrams: CHÊN: Thunder, arousing. CH'IEN: Heaven, active.

THE DECISION

Vigorous strength. Advantage comes from being firm and correct.

COMMENTARY

Here we see the great becoming strong. The trigram denoting strength directs that which denotes movement, indicating vigour. Advantage is shown proceeding from an attitude of firm correctness because what is great must also be correct. When correctness and greatness are combined, the character and tendencies of Heaven and earth are revealed.

Vigorous strength should be cultivated resolutely, but it is not in itself sufficient for the proper conduct of affairs. Strength should be held in subordination to the idea of the right, and be exerted only in harmony with it. Understanding of this truth leads to insight into the significance of all things.

THE IMAGE

Thunder (Chên) in Heaven (Ch'ien). The superior man does not take a step which might be in any way improper.

Nine in the first place: He reveals strength only in his toes. Progress will lead to evil.
Interpretation: He is not in a position to make his way by means of force.

Nine in the second place: With firm persistence there will be good fortune.
Interpretation: His future prospects are good.

Nine in the third place: The small man is provoked into using all his strength, even though his position is perilous. The superior man exercises restraint, although even for him temptation is great. If he gave way to it he would be like a goat butting against a fence until his horns become entangled.
Interpretation: Great caution is advised. In extreme situations the use of force will not restore balance; such self-indulgence will only make matters worse.

Nine in the fourth place: Firm persistence leads to good fortune; occasion for regret disappears. If he proceeds cautiously his strength will produce good effects. The hedge opens before him and his horns are freed from their entanglement. His strength is like that which resides in the axle of a great wagon.
Interpretation: Careful advance will lead to the removal of obstructions and difficulties. His real strength should not be revealed openly, but should be kept hidden in reserve like the great strength which lies in the axle of a heavy wagon: concealed, yet powerful.

Six in the fifth place: He sacrifices the ram easily. He will have no regret.
Interpretation: Being in a secure position, he relaxes and loses his ram-like alertness. Despite this, he will have no cause to repent. He who is in a position of strength can afford to relax.

Six in the sixth position: A ram butts against a hedge, unable to either advance or retreat. Nothing is of advantage. Yet such a difficulty brings good fortune.

Interpretation: He is like a ram butting futilely against a hedge; nothing he can do will further his aims, yet if his predicament leads to an awareness of the need for restraint there may yet be good fortune.

Hexagram 35

CHIN

PROGRESS

The trigrams: LI: Fire, clinging. K'UN: Earth, responsive.

THE DECISION

Progress. Because of the prince's service to his country he is presented with many horses, and is received in audience by the king three times in one day!

COMMENTARY

Here we have the bright sun appearing above the earth. The symbol of docile responsiveness clings to that of great brightness; the weak line progresses to the ruling position of the hexagram (the fifth line). All this gives us the idea of the successful prince who is presented with numerous horses and received by the king three times in a single day.

His advance is like that of the sun, shining more and more until it reaches high noon.

THE IMAGE

The bright sun (Li) comes forth above the earth (K'un). The superior man too shines brightly, because of his radiant virtue.

THE LINES

Six in the first place: He seeks to advance, but is held back. If he is firm and persevering he will have good fortune. If he is not trusted he should remain open-hearted and generous in his relationships; then he will avoid error.

Interpretation: He wishes to advance, but as his superior does not yet have confidence in him he is restrained. He should cultivate tolerance and a calm mind.

Six in the second place: He appears to be advancing, but yet is sorrowful. If he be firm and correct he will attain good fortune. This blessing will come from his grandmother.

Interpretation: His good fortune will come through the good offices of a motherly person in authority.

Six in the third place: He is trusted by all around him. He will have no cause for regret.

Interpretation: An atmosphere of mutual trust and common aim binds them together.

Nine in the fourth place: He moves quickly in the manner of a small rodent. If he persists in this reckless manner he will endanger himself.

Interpretation: Scurrying around in an undignified manner does not make for real progress. If he perseveres in such unseemly acts the outcome will be unfortunate.

Six in the fifth place: All occasion for regret disappears. Let him not concern himself about whether or not he will succeed. To advance will be fortunate and favourable in every way.

Interpretation: He holds steadfastly to his correct course, indifferent to the outcome. But events are so disposed that he is, and will continue to be, crowned with success.

Nine in the sixth place: He advances with extended horns, intent on punishing the rebels. Such a use of force on one's own people is risky; however correct he may be, he will have occasion for regret.

Interpretation: Great restraint must be observed if good fortune is to be attained.

Hexagram 36

MING I

HIDING OF THE LIGHT

The trigrams: K'UN: Earth, responsive. LI: Fire, clinging.

THE DECISION

Hiding of the light. In times of difficulty it is of advantage to remain firm and correct in one's actions.

COMMENTARY

Here brightness (Li) enters into the midst of the earth (K'un). The lower trigram denotes one who is intelligent and accomplished; the upper trigram one who is docile and submissive. Such a one was King Wên, who retained these qualities even while involved in great difficulties.

He who would turn his adversities to the best possible advantage must hide his bright qualities. A case in point was that of Prince Chi, who, amidst the difficulties of his House, was able to maintain his true will.

The good and intelligent minister goes forward in the service of his country, despite the fact that the throne is occupied by a weak and unsympathetic ruler. Under such conditions the superior man hides his virtues while inwardly remaining true to them.

THE IMAGE

The light (Li) is hidden inside the earth (K'un). When governing men the superior man reveals his wisdom by not seeking to display it openly.

Nine in the first place: He flies, but with drooping wings. Following his true course with great perseverance he fasts for three days without giving it a thought. People speak of him with derision.

Interpretation: He receives a serious set-back as soon as he sets out. All he can do is retire for a time and evade the obstacles before him. Reconciled to this, he accepts the privations imposed on him by fate; but those around can only criticize him for his failing in his aim.

Six in the second place: Although wounded in the thigh, he mounts a swift horse and saves himself, keeping still to his purpose.

Interpretation: Although his movements are impaired, he is not disabled and can continue along his course.

Nine in the third place: While hunting in the south he captures the chief of his enemies. But he is not over-eager to put everything right at once; he is able to restrain himself from acting prematurely.

Interpretation: Unexpected good fortune lies ahead, but one must not allow one's good judgement to be upset by elation. Deep-seated wrongs cannot be set right in a moment.

Six in the fourth place: He enters his enemy's territory as if into the left side of a man's belly, and sees there the ruler as if he were a black heart. Hiding his true identity, he is able to escape undetected.

Interpretation: He is given the opportunity to see the true nature of those opposing him, without placing himself in a vulnerable position.

Six in the fifth place: He acts like Prince Chi, who persisted in the right course of action even when trapped and wounded. The hidden light of his virtue still persists.

Interpretation: In times of great danger supreme firmness is required if one is to survive. One must be as a light burning in darkness.

Six in the sixth place: There is no light, but only darkness. He has ascended into the sky, now he will descend into the earth.
Interpretation: This is the fate of the ruler who opposes the minister willing to offer him good and intelligent service. Instead of becoming as the sun, casting light over everything from his vantage-point in the sky, he is like the sun hidden beneath the earth.

Hexagram 37

CHIA JÊN

THE FAMILY

The trigrams: SUN: Wind, gentle. LI: Fire, clinging.

THE DECISION

The family. The most important rule in family life is that the wife should be firm and correct in all her actions.

COMMENTARY

Here the wife occupies her proper place in the lower trigram, and the man has his correct place in the upper trigram. When man and woman occupy their rightful places they reflect the correct positions of Heaven and earth.

In this hexagram we see the idea of an authoritative ruler, represented here by parental authority.

Let the father be indeed father, and the son son; let the elder brother be indeed elder brother, and the younger brother younger brother; let the husband be indeed husband, and the wife wife; then will the family be in its proper state. Bring the family to that state, and all under Heaven will be established.

The proper regulation of the family is effected mainly by the co-operation between husband and wife in their respective spheres. If such regulation is carried over into the governing of the realm – that is, the relationship between the ruler and his people – then good order is assured.

Wind (Sun) issuing from fire (Li). The superior man regards the truth of things when he speaks, and is consistent in his thoughts.

THE LINES

Nine in the first place: He establishes regulations in his household. Regret will disappear.
Interpretation: Strict rules are necessary in the government of the family. Regulations must be established and their observance strictly insisted on.

Six in the second place: She takes nothing to herself, but occupies her own place, seeing to the preparation of the food. Through her firm correctness there will be good fortune.
Interpretation: One must concentrate on immediate tasks and leave larger issues until a more appropriate time.

Nine in the third place: He treats the members of his household with stern severity. There will be occasion for regret, even peril, but also good fortune. Facetiousness on the part of the wife and children will lead to regret.
Interpretation: It is better to be too severe than to be lax and indulgent.

Six in the fourth place: She enriches the family. There will be great good fortune.
Interpretation: The wife controls the domestic accounts, and by careful management brings wealth into the home.

Nine in the fifth place: The influence of the king is extended to his family. There need be no anxiety; good fortune is on its way.
Interpretation: The ruler restrains his power and uses his strength wisely for the benefit of all his subjects.

Nine in the sixth place: He is sincere and looks like a king. In the end there will be good fortune.

Interpretation: His sincerity gives him the dignified appearance of a king. Any abuse of his power would lead him into a mistaken display of stern severity, but his self-control and correct behaviour can only be fortunate in its outcome.

Hexagram 38

K'UEI

OPPOSITES

The trigrams: LI: Fire, clinging. TUI: Lake, joyful.

THE DECISION

Opposites. Although conditions of major opposition prevail, in small matters there will be success.

COMMENTARY

Here we have fire moving upwards, and water moving downwards. They are like two sisters living together, whose wills do not move in the same direction.

The lower trigram signifies harmonious satisfaction, and is attached to the upper trigram which signifies bright intelligence; the weak line has progressed until it occupies the central position in the upper trigram, from whence it responds to the strong lines below. This indicates that in small matters there will be good fortune.

Heaven and earth are separate and apart, but the work which they do unites them. Man and woman are separate and apart, but their common aims bring them together. There are great divisions between all beings, but they are related through their actions. The outcome of such separation is great indeed!

Division, misunderstanding, and mistrust abound throughout the country, and men are alienated from one another. But even such a major catastrophe can be put right in small ways, thus paving the way for the redeeming of the whole.

THE IMAGE

Fire (Li) above the lake (Tui). The superior man, even when others agree among themselves and act as one, is still kept apart from them by his superior integrity.

THE LINES

Nine in the first place: Occasion for regret will disappear. He has lost his horses, but let him not seek for them; they will return of their own accord. Though he mixes with evil men, they do not influence him.

Interpretation: What has been lost cannot be restored by force; he must be patient and wait for it to return in the fullness of time. In the same way, one cannot convert evil men by force, but given time one's good may overcome their evil, and will at least help to silence their slander.

Nine in the second place: He meets his lord unexpectedly in a by-way. There will be no error.

Interpretation: Such a chance meeting of opposites can be valuable, and may lead to an exchange of views and a better understanding.

Six in the third place: His carriage is dragged back and his oxen are denied passage and pushed back. He is forced into having his head shaved and his nose cut off. This is not a good beginning, but there will be a good end.

Interpretation: His troubles, though severe in the extreme, will not be without end.

Nine in the fourth place: At first he stands alone amidst the prevailing opposition and general disunion. But he meets with a good man, and they combine their sincere aims. Their position is perilous, but no mistake is incurred.

Interpretation: Mutual understanding and sympathy help to resolve opposition. Although danger threatens on every side, an auspicious start is made.

He draws his bow, then lowers it as he sees before him not an enemy but a near relative

Six in the fifth place: Occasion for regret will disappear. His relative bites through the skin. When he goes forward, what error can there be?
Interpretation: With the help of his own inner virtue he bites through his difficulties as if he were biting through a piece of skin. When he is united within himself in this fashion, how can he commit any error?

Nine in the sixth place: He stands alone amidst the prevailing disunion. He seems to see a pig covered in mud, then a wagon full of spirits; he draws his bow, then lowers it as he sees before him not an enemy but a near relative. Moving forward he encounters gentle rain, followed by great good fortune.
Interpretation: His inner resources guide him through the terrors and contradictions before him until they are resolved and he is on the safe path to good fortune.

Hexagram 39

OBSTRUCTIONS

The trigrams: K'AN: Water, dangerous. KÊN: Mountain, immovable.

THE DECISION

Obstructions. Advantage will be found in the south and west, but not in the north and east. It will be favourable to meet with the great man. Firm persistence brings good fortune.

COMMENTARY

This hexagram denotes difficulty. The trigram denoting danger lies above. If he can see the danger and halt his advance towards it, he is wise indeed.

Advantage will be found in the south and west because the strong line occupies the fifth place. There will be no advantage in the north and east because the power of those directions is exhausted. Advancing to meet the great man will lead to achievement.

Because the lines (other than the first) are in the positions appropriate to them, firm correctness will bring good fortune and resolve the difficulties of the kingdom. Great indeed is the work to be done at this time.

If obstructions are to give way to good fortune, consistent effort through all adversities is required. In the case of the superior man such difficulties can be turned to good account. External stresses help to reveal weaknesses within which would otherwise go unremedied.

THE IMAGE

Water (K'an) on the mountain (Kên). The superior man examines himself and nurtures his inner virtue.

THE LINES

Six in the first place: Advancing will lead to greater obstruction. Remaining still will bring praise.
Interpretation: If he advances he will not be able to cope with the difficulties of his situation, but will find himself overwhelmed. Let him wait for a more suitable time.

Six in the second place: The king's minister struggles with obstruction upon obstruction through no fault of his own, and without thought of personal advantage.
Interpretation: He is duty bound to pursue his course, and cannot delay. He must move straight ahead and try to overcome obstructions head on.

Nine in the third place: He advances, but only into greater difficulties. He is forced to a standstill, then has to turn back.
Interpretation: Here there is no advantage to be gained by struggling courageously. His cause is best served by retreating.

Six in the fourth place: He advances, but to still greater difficulties. Pausing will be of advantage.
Interpretation: Too weak to succeed alone, he cultivates his loyal attachment to the king and waits for the time when he will be required to act. Restraint on his part will allow adequate support to gather.

Nine in the fifth place: While struggling with the greatest difficulties, his friends arrive to help him.
Interpretation: He is seen to attack a major obstruction alone, and others rush to his assistance. Such united efforts lead to success.

Six in the sixth place: Advancing only leads to obstructions; pausing leads to great good fortune. It is advisable to see the great man.

Interpretation: Remaining still while seeking the wise counsel of a great man will bring powerful friends to his aid.

Hexagram 40

ESCAPE

The trigrams: CHÊN: Thunder, arousing. K'AN: Water, dangerous.

THE DECISION

Escape. Advantage will be found in the south and the west. If no further expeditions are called for, good fortune will come from returning home. If more are called for, a speedy settlement of them will be best.

COMMENTARY

Here the trigram depicting danger is confronted by that depicting powerful arousal. By movement there is an escape from peril.

Movement towards the south and west will win everyone to his cause. Returning home will enable him to follow a balanced way once more. The early completion of urgent tasks will ensure success.

When Heaven and earth are freed from the grip of winter, thunder and rain commence. As a result the buds of the plants and trees that produce fruit of all kinds begin to burst.

Great indeed are the occurrences of this time! The sooner things fall into their old channels the better. The new masters of the kingdom should not be too anxious to change the old ways and customs.

THE IMAGE

Thunder (Chên) and rain (K'an) bring release. The superior man forgives errors and deals gently with crimes.

THE LINES

Six in the first place: He commits no error.
Interpretation: His problems are resolved; there is no longer any conflict.

Nine in the second place: While out hunting he kills three foxes with one perfect yellow arrow. Firm correctness will bring good fortune.
Interpretation: Through wise persistence he overcomes his opponents with ease.

Six in the third place: He travels in a carriage, with a porter to handle his baggage. Such behaviour will tempt robbers to attack him. However firm and correct he might try to be, there will be cause for regret.
Interpretation: He cannot protect himself nor accomplish anything worth while. Needless ostentation invites the approach of danger.

Nine in the fourth place: Remove your toes. Friends in whom you can trust will then approach.
Interpretation: He removes hangers-on from his immediate circle, thus allowing true friends to approach and be taken into his confidence.

Six in the fifth place: The superior man removes hampering restrictions which are contrary to the peace and good order of the kingdom, thus gaining the confidence of even small men. There will be good fortune.
Interpretation: Such actions require great single-mindedness if they are to succeed.

Six in the sixth place: The prince looses an arrow from his bow and hits a falcon sitting on top of a high wall. The effect of this action will be in every way advantageous.

Interpretation: He removes the most powerful of his enemies and escapes from their domination.

Hexagram 41

DECREASE

The trigrams: KÊN: Mountain, immovable. TUI: Lake, joyful.

THE DECISION

Decrease. A decrease of what is in excess brings great good
fortune if it is carried out with sincerity. It results in freedom
from error, firm correctness which can be maintained, and
advantage in every action that is undertaken. In what circumstances should this gainful decrease be employed? Even when
making sacrifices to Heaven, two baskets of grain are a better
offering than insincere munificence.

COMMENTARY

Here the lower trigram is diminished and the upper added to.
The power of the hexagram proceeds upwards.

There is a time when the strong should be diminished and
the weak strengthened. Diminution and increase, fullness and
emptiness; all these take place in harmony with the conditions
of the time.

Every diminution of what we hold in excess brings it into
accordance with right and reason. Let there be sincerity in
doing this and it will lead to the happiest results. It will lead
to success in great things. Even if the decrease be very small,
yet it will be accepted, as in the most solemn sacrifice.

THE IMAGE

The lake (Tui) at the foot of the mountain (Kên). The superior man restrains his anger and controls his animal desires.

THE LINES

Nine in the first place: He leaves his own affairs and hurries to help another. There is no error in this, so long as he realizes what he is giving up in order to do it.
Interpretation: Careful deliberation is required before making such a sacrifice.

Nine in the second place: To gain advantage from the situation he should be firm and correct; rash movement on his part would lead to evil. He can give to others without taking from himself.
Interpretation: Slow deliberation is advised.

Six in the third place: When three walk together, interests conflict and one must go. When he walks alone he is able to find a companion with whom he will not conflict.
Interpretation: It is better to travel alone at the outset. Alliances made at this time would not be favourable.

Six in the fourth place: By decreasing the number of faults which afflict him he makes it possible for others to help him. Thus he attains happiness. There will be no error.
Interpretation: He must become aware of his faults and set about eradicating them before offers of help can be looked for.

Six in the fifth place: He is given great quantities of tortoiseshells by one who will accept no refusal. There will be great good fortune.
Interpretation: Such good fortune cannot be decreased in any way; it is a gift from on high.

Nine in the sixth place: He gives increase to others without diminishing his own resources. There will be no error, and if he exercises firm perseverance he will have great good fortune and advantage for himself in every move he makes. Innumerable ministers will come to serve him.

Interpretation: Supreme good fortune! Such benefits favour not only him who receives them, but the whole of the people.

Hexagram 42

I

INCREASE

The trigrams: SUN: Wind, gentle. CHÊN: Thunder, arousing.

THE DECISION

Increase. There will be advantage in every undertaking. It will be advantageous even to cross the great water.

COMMENTARY

Here the upper trigram is diminished and the lower added to. As a result of this the satisfaction of the people is without limit. What descends from above reaches all below, so great and brilliant is its virtue.

The central position of each trigram is occupied by the correct line, suggesting the scattering of blessings which is described above. The advice concerning crossing the great water is suggested by the strong position of the upper trigram.

Daily advancement can be made to an unlimited extent, through exercise of the qualities of movement and gentleness. Heaven dispenses its bounty and earth produces its fruits in unrestricted profusion.

If the ruler strives to dispense benefits to the people and increase the general level of prosperity, he will be given loyalty in return. Thus he will be able to do great things.

THE IMAGE

Wind (Sun) and thunder (Chên). The superior man proceeds towards what is good when he sees it; when he perceives what is bad he turns from it.

THE LINES

Nine in the first place: It will be advantageous for him to move forward with great confidence. His success will make his earlier rashness be forgotten. There will be no blame.
Interpretation: The time is now right for commencing great enterprises.

Six in the second place: He is given many tortoise-shells by one who is insistent in his generosity. If he perseveres in being firm and correct there will be good fortune. The king who presents his offerings to Heaven in a lavish fashion increases the good fortune of all.
Interpretation: The time is favourable for Heaven to confer its benefits. But he should maintain his calmness and equilibrium even in such joyful circumstances.

Six in the third place: He increases his wealth by doubtful means, but as he is unaware of his wrong he remains without blame. If he is sincere and treads the narrow path of rectitude he will secure recognition of his true worth, like one who announces himself to the prince by wearing his tablet of rank.
Interpretation: His dealings are open to criticism, but as he acts innocently, without guile, he will escape censure.

Six in the fourth place: He follows a correct course of action and thus gains the ear of the prince. Such is the trust placed in him that he is relied on to carry out important tasks; even that of relocating the Imperial capital!
Interpretation: His actions gain him the confidence of those in authority over him.

He is given many tortoise-shells by one who is insistent in his generosity

Nine in the fifth place: With a sincere heart he seeks to benefit all beneath him. Without question the outcome will be fortunate in the extreme. All below will, with sincere hearts, acknowledge his goodness.

Interpretation: He acts from a position of great strength and the universe supports him. Therefore he cannot fail.

Nine in the sixth place: He concentrates his powers on the increase of himself, but thinking to benefit those beneath him. Therefore none will support him and many will seek to assail him. He observes no regular ruling in the ordering of his heart; there will be evil.

Interpretation: By abusing the opportunities he is given he forfeits their benefits, although he means well.

Hexagram 43

RENEWED ADVANCE

The trigrams: TUI: Lake, joyful. CH'IEN: Heaven, active.

THE DECISION

Renewed advance. He who resolves to proceed must first exhibit
the culprit's guilt in the Royal court, appealing for sympathy
in an earnest and sincere manner. At the same time he must be
conscious of the peril his actions place him in. Moreover he
must make his followers understand, as if he were speaking to
the people of his own city, how unwillingly he takes up arms.
Then let him proceed and he will be accompanied by good
fortune.

COMMENTARY

Here the strong displaces the weak. Strength conjoined with
joyfulness results in harmonious displacement.

The scene in the Royal court is suggested by the single weak
line resting on the five strong ones. The appreciation of his
danger makes his success all the more brilliant.

If he takes up arms too readily his fund of good will cannot
last long. When the advance of the strong lines has been completed, progress will come to an end.

He must denounce the wrong-doer, seek to awaken general
sympathy for his cause, and at the same time proceed with his
enterprise, being fully aware of its difficulty and danger. He

must achieve his aims by the power of his character more than by the use of force.

THE IMAGE

The lake (Tui) rising up to Heaven (Ch'ien). The superior man bestows riches on those below him and does not allow his wealth to accumulate unused.

THE LINES

Nine in the first place: He starts out proudly, but without adequate preparation. He moves forward, but will not succeed. He cannot avoid recrimination.
Interpretation: An advance at this time will not be favourable in its outcome.

Nine in the second place: He is alert and apprehensive as he appeals for help. Hostile moves may be made against him during the night, but he need not be anxious about them.
Interpretation: Because he is armed and prepared for any eventuality, he can afford to be confident.

Nine in the third place: He advances in a strong and determined manner. Because he reveals his purpose too openly there will be evil. But the superior man who is determined to repress the criminal will walk alone, in an unruffled manner, through the rain that falls against him, until even his own associates will believe he has gone over to the enemy. In the end no blame will be laid against him.
Interpretation: Conditions are such that a direct attack on the forces of evil will not succeed. Cautious and diplomatic moves are required if an advance is to be made. He who undertakes to follow such a difficult and unpopular course is sure to be misunderstood, but as his actions are proper he will in the end be shown to have been right.

Nine in the fourth place: He walks slowly and with difficulty because he has been flayed. If only he could act as if he were a sheep, and suffer to be led by his companion, he might still accomplish something. But he will not listen to advice, and alone he can do nothing.

Interpretation: Although suffering from past mistakes, he still will not listen to wise advice and is unwilling to deflect from his predetermined course.

Nine in the fifth place: He pursues his chosen way with the utmost determination, like a bed of ground-hugging herbs which, though frail, yet survive. Because of his tenacity his actions can lead to no error or blame.

Interpretation: Great opposition seems unavoidable, yet determination will see him through.

Six in the sixth place: He finds himself in a vulnerable position without any helpers on whom he can call. His end will be evil.

Interpretation: Lack of necessary caution and preparation renders him open to misfortune. One must remain aware of evil even when it is not apparent.

Hexagram 44

KOU

SUDDEN ENCOUNTERS

The trigrams: CH'IEN: Heaven, active. SUN: Wind, gentle.

THE DECISION

Sudden encounters. A bold, strong woman appears on the scene. One should not contract a marriage with such a female.

COMMENTARY

Here the weak line encounters the strong lines suddenly. A marriage entered into now would not last long.

An encounter between Heaven and earth results in the creation of all natural things. When strong lines are in the central and correct positions, good government will prevail throughout the world.

The importance of what must be done at this time is great indeed!

The small and unworthy man begins to insinuate himself into the government of the realm. If his influence is not checked it will continue to grow, displacing one good man after another, until he is able to fill the vacant seats with others like himself.

The infiltration of such men must be resisted.

THE IMAGE

Wind (Sun) blowing under the sky (Ch'ien). The ruler issues his decrees and has them proclaimed throughout the four quarters of the kingdom.

Six in the first place: He should be kept back, as if he were a carriage with its brake on. Firm correctness at this time will bring good fortune. If he is allowed to move in any direction, evil will appear. He will be like a lean and dangerous pig which is sure to keep leaping out.

Interpretation: If he can be kept back, firm government and order may proceed. But powerful restraints need be imposed on him if this is to happen.

Nine in the second place: The inferior men are restrained like fish in a bag, thus forestalling any danger. It would not be well to let such fish be given to one's guests!

Interpretation: His enemies are in his power; but he must guard them carefully.

Nine in the third place: He proceeds with difficulty, like one who has been flayed. His position is fraught with danger, but despite this he will commit no great error.

Interpretation: Although he has suffered a great set-back, he manages to proceed slowly along the correct path.

Nine in the fourth place: The inferior men have escaped from restraint, like fish from a bag. This will give rise to evil.

Interpretation: The evil comes through a lack of vigilance. Such carelessness is not easily rectified.

Nine in the fifth place: The gourd is hidden beneath the leaves that are wrapped around it. Then it falls as if from Heaven.

Interpretation: Unexpected blessings can shortly be expected to arrive. If the superior man conceals his brilliant qualities he will be rewarded for his restraint in the fullness of time.

Nine in the sixth place: When they approach he lowers his

horns and turns them away. There will be occasion for regret, but no error.

Interpretation: Though isolated and unable to act with good effect, yet he manages to keep himself aloof from the lesser men who surround him.

The gourd is hidden beneath the leaves that are wrapped around it

Hexagram 45

COLLECTING TOGETHER

The trigrams: TUI: Lake, joyful. K'UN: Earth, responsive.

THE DECISION

Collecting together. The king approaches the ancestral temple. It will be advantageous to see the great man. There will be progress and success, though firm perseverance is required if the most is to be made of this auspicious time. Great sacrifices will be conducive to good fortune; movement in any direction will be advantageous.

COMMENTARY

Here we have docile obedience added to joyful satisfaction. The central position of the upper trigram is occupied by a strong line, therefore we have the idea of collecting together.

The king repairs to his ancestral temple and there presents his offerings with the utmost piety.

Meeting with the great man will result in the collecting together of forces to further what is right and proper.

By carrying out great sacrifices and by moving in any direction he will be acting in accordance with the will of Heaven.

By observing how collecting together takes place, we can see the inner workings of Heaven and earth and of all things.

When a state of convivial union exists between the king and his ministers, and between high and low, general good fortune

173

will prevail. If such a state is to continue, the ceremonies of religion must be observed and a sage must occupy the throne of Heaven.

THE IMAGE

The lake (Tui) rises over the earth (K'un). The superior man sees that his weapons are always in good repair, in order that he might be ready for the unforeseen.

THE LINES

Six in the first place: He has a sincere desire for union, but is unable to attain it because of the disorder that surrounds him. If he cries out for help, his tears will be replaced by smiles. Temporary difficulties should not be minded; there will be no error if he proceeds.
Interpretation: Though his future looks dark, help is at hand. All he has to do is ask.

Six in the second place: He is led along the right path. There will be good fortune and freedom from error. Because of his sincerity even a small sacrifice (such as that offered at the time of the Vernal Equinox) will be acceptable.
Interpretation: A hidden tide is operating in his affairs; if he opens himself to it he will attain good fortune.

Six in the third place: He strives after union, yet sadly finds himself unable to achieve it. If he continues his efforts he will not be in error. but may have some small cause for regret.
Interpretation: He will accomplish his object, though not without difficulty.

Nine in the fourth place: Great good fortune approaches, and he need fear no blame.
Interpretation: But caution is still indicated.

Nine in the fifth place: He successfully unites all beneath him without error on his part. But all do not yet have confidence in him, so he must persist in his virtuous conduct in order to overcome such doubts.

Interpretation: He achieves his aim, but further effort is needed before he can consolidate his triumph and consider his task done.

Six in the sixth place: He sighs and weeps, but there will be no error.

Interpretation: He is in a solitary position, unable to further his policy of collecting together. But as he is working along the right lines he will be preserved from falling into error.

Hexagram 46

ASCENDING

The trigrams: K'UN: Earth, responsive. SUN: Wind, gentle.

THE DECISION

Ascending. Great progress and success. He need suffer no anxiety when seeking an interview with the great man. Proceeding towards the south will be fortunate.

COMMENTARY

Here we see the weak line ascending at the appropriate time. The trigram denoting flexibility is joined to that denoting docility. A strong line occupies the central place of the lower trigram, indicating that there will be great progress and success.

Seeking to meet with the great man will give him grounds for congratulation; by proceeding towards the south his aim will be carried out.

Ascending denotes the rise of a worthy officer to a place of distinction. He attains his position of eminence because he displays forcefulness tempered by modesty. The time is now favourable for his advancement; those in superior positions will look on him with favour. The south is the region of warmth and joyful activity, and signifies his goal.

THE IMAGE

Trees and vegetation (Sun) ascending the earth (K'un). The superior man cultivates his virtue, accumulating small benefits until he has achieved merit which is high and great.

THE LINES

Six in the first place: He ascends towards the welcome of those who are above him. There will be great good fortune.
Interpretation: His progress will be unimpeded because he is looked on with favour.

Nine in the second place: His sincerity is of the kind which makes even a small sacrifice, such as that of the Vernal Equinox, acceptable. There will be no error.
Interpretation: The strong officer serves a weak ruler; he could not do that unless he was sincere and devotedly loyal.

Nine in the third place: He ascends, as into a large city.
Interpretation: He advances fearlessly. Rather more modesty would be in order.

Six in the fourth place: On behalf of the king he presents offerings on mount Chi. There will be good fortune, and no error.
Interpretation: The king confides in his minister and raises him to the highest distinction as a feudal lord. His ambitions are fulfilled.

Six in the fifth place: In a ceremonious manner he ascends step by step to the peak. If he is to reach the point of greatest dignity, perfect correctness is called for. Then good fortune will be his.
Interpretation: He must not allow his swift ascent to turn his head; calm progress and careful attention to detail are still required if he is to make the most of his opportunity.

Six in the sixth place: He proceeds blindly upwards. It will be advantageous for him to maintain his firm persistence.

Interpretation: His ascent is reckless and foolish. The forcefulness that has brought him success is about to involve him in loss. Only the most exact cultivation of a proper sense of modesty can save him from the consequences of his foolhardy actions.

Hexagram 47

K'UN

EXHAUSTING RESTRICTION

The trigrams: TUI: Lake, joyful. K'AN: Water, dangerous.

THE DECISION

Exhausting restriction. There may yet be progress and success. For the really great man there will be good fortune. He will fall into no error, but merely making speeches will not help prevailing difficulties.

COMMENTARY

Here the strong lines are covered and obscured by the weak. That which is dangerous is joined to that which is joyful. He who, though in grave difficulties, yet succeeds in following his aim is truly a superior man.

That the great man will have good fortune is shown by the placing of strong lines in the centre of both trigrams. To rely on arguments or pleading is to cultivate disaster.

When good fortune departs, all one can do is submit. But by retaining one's integrity and optimism the groundwork for future success may be laid. Only a truly great man is able to do this without error, when his position is akin to that of a tree which is not allowed to spread its branches. Despite all, his efforts will ensure his ultimate good fortune.

THE IMAGE

No water (K'an) in the lake (Tui). The superior man will sacrifice even his life to fulfil his purpose.

THE LINES

Six in the first place: He is restricted by the branches of a barren tree. He enters a dark valley and for three years has no hope of deliverance.
Interpretation: The exhausting effect of adverse circumstances can lead to the path of dark despair. This must be combated at an early stage if serious setbacks are to be avoided.

Nine in the second place: He is troubled by an excess of food and drink. A noble wearing red knee-covers approaches, and it will be advisable to offer him suitable sacrifices. Activity on his part will lead to misfortune, even though he will remain free from blame.
Interpretation: Over-indulgence leads to error. Self-discipline is needed, if influential help is to be gained. Moving ahead too quickly, though in the right spirit, will not help matters. Let him cultivate sincerity and calmness, and all will be well.

Six in the third place: He is confronted by frowning rocks and has only thorns to hang on to. Entering his house, he cannot find his wife. There will be evil.
Interpretation: Insurmountable obstructions bar his progress. Hopes prove false, and his whole existence is in a stage of great instability and danger.

Nine in the fourth place: He proceeds very slowly, and is restricted by a golden carriage. There will be occasion for regret, but the end will be good.
Interpretation: Placing his faith in material possessions at this time may retard his progress rather than assist it.

Nine in the fifth place: His nose and feet are cut off. He is held back by a minister wearing purple knee-bands. It will be well for him to offer sincere sacrifice if satisfaction is to be attained.
Interpretation: He can expect no success from any quarter, high or low. Those who may be expected to help will not do so, and may indeed hinder him. Humility and correct behaviour are necessary if he is to reach better fortune later.

Six in the sixth place: He is bound as if by creepers, or as if he was hanging in a high and dangerous position. He moves unsteadily and says to himself, 'If I move I shall regret it.' If true regret is felt, the way will be opened for the approach of good fortune.
Interpretation: A realization of the nature of his mistakes will open the way for their correction.

Hexagram 48

THE WELL

The trigrams: K'AN: Water, dangerous. SUN: Wind, gentle.

THE DECISION

The well. The site of a town may be changed, but its well cannot be moved. The well is never exhausted; although people come, draw water, and enjoy the benefit of it, the water level stays almost constant. But if the rope be too short or the water jug broken, there will be evil.

COMMENTARY

A jug is put into the water and the water is raised up; such is the nature of a well. The well supplies nourishment without being itself exhausted.

The stability of the well – it keeps its position even when the town is moved – is symbolized by the placing of strong lines in the centre of both trigrams.

The possible shortness of the rope suggests that one's aims may be too ambitious; the breaking of the water jug indicates definite failure.

The relationship between the well and those living round it is like that of the good government and its subjects. The well remains the same through all the changes of society; it can always be depended on both for refreshment and for use in agriculture. The value of a well is in proportion to the amount of water that can be drawn from it. If rulers could appreciate the lesson of the well they would benefit both themselves and their people. The state should be ordered in such a way that the people can have access to the benefits of their rulers without hindrance; otherwise they will be like he who goes to the well only to find the rope too short or the pitcher broken.

THE IMAGE

Water (K'an) over wood (Sun). The superior man comforts the people and inspires them to help one another.

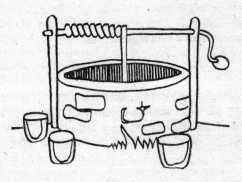

The well

THE LINES

Six in the first place: The well is so muddy that men will not drink from it. An old well attracts neither birds nor animals.
Interpretation: Many men in positions of authority are like such a well: corrupt, useless, ignored.

Nine in the second place: The well is breached, letting the water and fish in it both escape. Water leaks from the broken jug.
Interpretation: The ministers of a country should be able and willing to administer the state in a proper manner, but their talents are often misapplied or simply wasted.

183

Nine in the third place: The well has been cleaned, but not put into use. This is a saddening state of affairs. If only the king were wiser all might benefit.

Interpretation: When talented people are neglected, it gives cause for sorrow.

Six in the fourth place: The lining of the well is firm and well laid. There will be no error.

Interpretation: He is not to be condemned, but neither should he be praised. Although taking care of himself, he as yet does nothing for others.

Nine in the fifth place: The water of the well is cool and limpid, like the water from a cool stream.

Interpretation: It is drawn up and performs a useful function. In a similar way the good ruler serves his people.

Six in the sixth place: The water is drawn to the top of the well, which lies uncovered and open to all. This can be likened to the true sincerity which leads on to great good fortune.

Interpretation: Some supreme achievement is indicated here.

Hexagram 49

KÔ

REVOLUTION

The trigrams: TUI: Lake, joyful. LI: Fire, clinging.

THE DECISION

Revolution. Revolution is only believed in when it has been accomplished. There will be great progress and success. Advantage will come from being firm and correct, removing all occasion for regret.

COMMENTARY

Here water and fire extinguish each other, like two daughters who dwell together in enmity and discord. Hence the name revolution.

Revolution must take place before the necessity for it can be widely recognized. Cultivated intelligence is the basis of joyful satisfaction; it leads to great progress and success. When revolution takes place at an appropriate time, it leads to the ending of regret.

Heaven and earth undergo their changes, and the four seasons complete their revolution. T'ang and Wu led insurrections according to the will of Heaven and in response to the wishes of men. Great indeed is the significance of such a time.

Change of any kind is generally viewed by people with suspicion and dislike; therefore it must be instigated gradually. When change is necessary, it will only be approved after it has been seen to work. A proved necessity beforehand, and a firm correctness throughout: these are the conditions under which revolutions can be successfully brought about.

THE IMAGE

Fire (Li) in the midst of the lake (Tui). The superior man regulates the calendar and makes clear the seasons and times.

THE LINES

Nine in the first place: He is bound as with thongs of yellow oxhide.
Interpretation: Revolution was begun too early, and he is unable to gain the assistance he needs.

Six in the second place: He makes changes after a proper lapse of time. Such action will be fortunate, and there need be no fear of error.
Interpretation: Thoughtful restraint will ensure good fortune.

Nine in the third place: His actions will result in evil. Though he be firm and correct, yet there will be peril. If he discusses his proposed action thoroughly with his colleagues before he acts, he will gain their necessary trust and support.
Interpretation: Prevailing conditions tempt him to act recklessly and make violent changes. Caution and careful planning are required.

Nine in the fourth place: Regret disappears. He has the trust of those around him, and changes he now makes will have a fortunate outcome.
Interpretation: Having secured general confidence, he may proceed.

Nine in the fifth place: The great man makes changes in the manner of a tiger changing its stripes. First he consults the oracle and then he acts, confident in the rightness of what he is doing.

Interpretation: The outcome of his actions can be likened to the bright stripes of the tiger which has changed its coat.

Six in the sixth place: The superior man makes changes as the leopard changes his spots, while small men alter their faces and show obedience. To proceed will lead to evil; remaining still, firmly and correctly, will bring good fortune.

Interpretation: Although the superior man can instigate changes in a natural manner, without causing an upset – in the way that a leopard quietly changes his spots – lesser men are advised to refrain from action. They should adapt themselves to the conditions of the time.

Hexagram 50

THE CAULDRON

The trigrams: LI: Fire, clinging. SUN: Wind, gentle.

THE DECISION

The cauldron. Great progress and success!

COMMENTARY

Here we have the cauldron; the trigram signifying wood enters into that signifying fire. This gives rise to the idea of cooking. The sages cooked their offerings before presenting them to the Lord of Heaven, and prepared great feasts to nourish the wise and virtuous.

The symbol of docile obedience is here added to that which denotes sharp hearing and clear-sightedness. The weak line has ascended to the central position in the upper trigram, and the firm lines respond to it; this suggests great progress and success.

The cauldron is used for cooking, and symbolizes nourishment. Therefore it furthers success. The nourishment of men of talent and virtue leads to great progress in the realm. The superior man strives to become as the contents of the cauldron, sacrificing himself in order that his good qualities might nourish other men.

THE IMAGE

Fire (Li) over wood (Sun). The superior man maintains his firm position and obeys the edicts of Heaven.

Six in the first place: The cauldron is inverted to remove decaying matter. There is no blame in taking a concubine for the son she will bear.

Interpretation: Extreme circumstances sometimes require unorthodox actions; carefully keeping to the path of conventional virtue is sometimes not enough. Overturning a cauldron or taking a concubine can be said to be blameworthy, but on occasion such actions are necessary.

Nine in the second place: The cauldron is filled with food. His enemies are frustrated and cannot harm him. Good fortune!

Interpretation: He is in a strong position; opposition is thwarted and his continued progress assured.

Nine in the third place: The handles of the cauldron have been removed, therefore it is hard to manoeuvre the vessel. The fat flesh of the pheasant is not eaten. But the coming of rain will end regret, bringing good fortune in the end.

Interpretation: An avoidable error will cause delay, resulting in the loss of a good opportunity. Fortunately this setback will not have a far-reaching effect, and success will finally be grasped.

Nine in the fourth place: The legs of the cauldron are broken. The prince's food is spilled and his person soiled. There will be misfortune.

Interpretation: A grave error of judgement is made by one unequal to the task entrusted to him. Trouble and blame will be the outcome.

Six in the fifth place: The cauldron has yellow handles with golden rings attached. There will be advantage through being firm and correct.

Interpretation: The ruler lends his power and virtue to those beneath him. Such co-operation will lead to happy results, but perseverance is still necessary.

Nine in the sixth place: The cauldron has rings of jade. There will be great good fortune, and every action will be advantageous.

Interpretation: Jade is very hard, but yet has a softness all its own. If he combines these qualities within himself, great good fortune is assured him and all will be well.

Hexagram 51

THUNDER

The trigrams: CHÊN: Thunder, arousing. CHÊN: Thunder, arousing.

THE DECISION

Thunder. Thunder signifies movement and success. When it crashes he will be found peering out at it with apprehension, yet nevertheless smiling and talking cheerfully. When the noise terrifies everyone within a hundred miles he will remain unperturbed, approaching the temple with his cup of sacrificial wine held safely in his hands.

COMMENTARY

Thunder suggests successful progress; the feeling of dread which it inspires leads to happiness, because its fearful upheaval is the prelude to a state of calm order.

Peals of thunder startle the distant and frighten those close at hand, but the cup of sacrificial wine is not upset because one appears who is qualified to maintain the ancestral temple and the altars of the gods of the land, and to preside at all sacrifices.

The superior man is aware of the dangers of the time, and by caution and careful regulation of his actions he may overcome them. His self-possession and sincere concentration on what is truly important will ensure his safety and success.

191

Repeated thunder (Chên). The superior man is fearful and apprehensive, cultivates his virtue and examines his faults.

THE LINES

Nine in the first place: Thunder approaches. He looks round and about cautiously, then smiles and talks cheerfully.
Interpretation: There will be good fortune.

Approaching the temple with his cup of sacrificial wine held safely in his hands

Six in the second place: The approaching thunder finds him in a perilous position. After due consideration he abandons his valuables and ascends to a lofty height. He need not search for the things he has lost; within seven days they will be returned to him.
Interpretation: If he can retreat from his hard-won position to a place of safety when danger threatens, and not seek to

hang on to what he has gained at all costs, all will effortlessly be returned to him when the danger has passed.

Six in the third place: The thunder catches him unawares, leaving him distraught and bewildered. But if it stimulates him into thunderous action of his own, he will avoid falling into error.
Interpretation: He must try to regain his composure sufficiently to take appropriate evading action. Violent conditions require violent remedies.

Nine in the fourth place: Startled by the thunder, he stumbles in the mud.
Interpretation: Unanticipated danger will cause him to make a serious error of judgement.

Six in the fifth place: He comes and goes amidst the peals of thunder, always in peril. But he may avoid the danger and accomplish his important business.
Interpretation: Although his position is vulnerable, he may yet achieve his aims.

Six in the sixth place: He looks around in breathless dismay as the thunder rolls, glancing about in trembling apprehension. If he tries to take action there will be evil. If he were to take precautions while the thunder was still far off he might avoid the danger, though his colleagues would still criticize him.
Interpretation: He must resign himself to the fact that the approaching setback is unavoidable. Precautions taken in advance will help minimize its effects, but he cannot completely avoid censure.

Hexagram 52

STILLNESS

The trigrams: KÊN: Mountain, immovable. KÊN: Mountain, immovable.

THE DECISION

Stillness. Keeping his back perfectly still, he loses all consciousness of his body. He walks in his courtyard but does not notice the people there. There will be no error.

COMMENTARY

This hexagram signifies coming to a halt. Resting when it is time to rest, and acting when it is time to act. When all movement and resting takes place at the appropriate times, one's progress is brilliant.

Here stillness occurs in its proper place. The upper and lower trigrams correspond to each other but do not interact; therefore it is said that he loses all consciousness of his body.

The various parts of the body all have uses outside themselves. Only the back has no external function. Like a mountain, all it has to do is remain in its place and stand straight and strong. We ought to keep still as the back does, free from the intrusion of selfish thoughts and external concerns. He who attains this stillness does not allow himself to be distracted from contemplation and the following of high principles. But he is not a recluse who keeps himself apart from others; his inward gaze is so steadfast that he is the same whether he is alone or in company.

THE IMAGE

Mountains (Kên) upon mountains. The superior man does not allow his thoughts to stray beyond his present situation.

THE LINES

Six in the first place: He keeps his toes still. There will be no error, but it will be advantageous for him to be persistently firm and correct.
Interpretation: Great caution is advised.

Keeping his back perfectly still, he loses all consciousness of his body

Six in the second place: He keeps the calves of his legs still. He cannot help the one he follows and is ill at ease, being frustrated in his aim.
Interpretation: Despite extreme provocation, he should refrain from premature action.

Nine in the third place: He keeps his loins still, divorcing his heart from bodily desires. But he is still in a perilous position, and his heart is enflamed with suppressed excitement.

Interpretation: Stillness imposed on the body by the mind before it is ready leads to psychic disorders. All aspects of oneself must be guided towards stillness at the same time if unbalance is to be avoided.

Six in the fourth place: He keeps his body at rest. There will be no error.

Interpretation: Having successfully trained all parts of himself he achieves stillness through all levels of his being.

Six in the fifth place: He stills his jaws, carefully disciplining his words. Occasion for regret will disappear.

Interpretation: Mental discipline as well as physical training is necessary.

Nine in the sixth place: Lovingly he maintains the stillness he has achieved. There will be good fortune.

Interpretation: By not relaxing when he has achieved his object, but instead maintaining his careful disipline as if it still lay ahead, he ensures that the fortunate state will continue.

Hexagram 53

CHIEN

GRADUAL ADVANCE

The trigrams: SUN: Wind, gentle. KÊN: Mountain, immovable.

THE DECISION

Gradual advance. The marriage of a young maiden brings good fortune. There will be advantage in being firm and correct.

COMMENTARY

The progress indicated here is like the fortunate marriage of a young lady. The lines advance to their correct places, indicating successful achievement.

Because he advances correctly, he is able to change conditions in his country for the better. This is indicated by the strong line which occupies the central position of the upper trigram.

From the joining together of mildness (Sun) and steadfastness (Kên) we see the start of inexhaustible forward movement.

The marriage of a young maiden takes place slowly, by means of many preliminary stages, all of which must be gone through in an orderly and correct manner. In such a fashion does a man gradually rise in the service of the state, following his ordained path like the wild goose which flies in its allotted place in the flock, heading towards the sun.

A tree (Sun) upon the mountain (Kên). The superior man first attains and then abides in his flawless virtue, guiding the people into paths of goodness.

The goose goes towards the trees, looking for a flat branch on which to alight

THE LINES

Six in the first place: The wild goose gradually approaches the shore. The young man is in danger, and will be spoken against. But there will be no error.

Interpretation: Following a correct course of action will involve him in criticism, but should be carried through nevertheless.

Six in the second place: The goose gradually approaches the large rocks, and eats and drinks in a happy manner. There will be good fortune.
Interpretation: He reaches a safe vantage-point, and may relax in peace.

Nine in the third place: The goose advances on to dry land. There will be misfortune, as when a husband sets off on an expedition and does not return, or a wife is pregnant and does not love her child. It is advantageous to withstand enemies.
Interpretation: Impetuous progress which does not take into account the feeling of others will result in evil. But the use of strength to protect others will be fortunate in its outcome.

Six in the fourth place: The goose goes towards the trees, looking for a flat branch on which to alight. There will be no error.
Interpretation: Advancing carefully, he seeks a place to rest. Being aware of his limitations, his humble endeavours will keep him from error.

Nine in the fifth place: The goose gradually advances to higher ground. There will be good fortune, as in the case of a wife who for three years cannot become pregnant, then succeeds.
Interpretation: Long denial will in due season give way to supreme success.

Nine in the sixth place: The goose gradually moves to the heights beyond. Its feathers can be used ceremonially, ensuring good fortune.
Interpretation: Having reached his goal he can stop pushing onwards. Instead he may use his accumulated wisdom for the good of all.

Hexagram 54

KUEI MEI

THE MARRYING MAIDEN

The trigrams: CHÊN: Thunder, arousing. TUI: Lake, joyful.

THE DECISION

The marrying maiden. Action will be evil; no advantage can come of it.

COMMENTARY

Here the great and righteous relationship between Heaven and earth is suggested. If Heaven and earth were to have no intercourse, things would not grow and flourish as they do. The marriage of a maiden signifies the end of her maidenhood and the start of her motherhood.

This hexagram combines joy and movement, suggesting the marriage of a young girl. Action will bring evil, because not all the lines are in appropriate places. There can be no advantage, because weak lines are mounted on strong ones.

It is as if a marriage were arranged by a maiden; she proceeding to her future husband's home instead of waiting for him to come to her. Earthly marriage is looked on with favour by Heaven as following the divine order, but when the weak becomes superior to the strong, only misfortune can follow. To ensure long-term success one must avoid mistakes at the beginning.

THE IMAGE

Thunder (Chên) over the waters (Tui). The superior man, his eyes on the far distant future, remains conscious of the mistakes that can be made in the present.

THE LINES

Nine in the first place: The maiden marries a man who already has one wife. Although she becomes a mere secondary wife, she is like the person with one leg who still manages to move forward. Such progress is fortunate.
Interpretation: Despite limitations, one's aims will not be completely restricted.

Nine in the second place: Although blind in one eye, she can see well enough. Advantage will come through acting with the single-mindedness of a hermit.
Interpretation: Great devotion to one's primary aim, despite major disadvantages, will ensure that adequate progress is made.

Six in the third place: She planned to be married, but being only a poor servant she is forced by circumstances into agreeing to become a concubine.
Interpretation: After the failure of a major ambition, lowering one's sights to a more realistic goal enables progress to be made.

Nine in the fourth place: Although of a marriageable age, she holds back. Although her marriage will thus be delayed, it will take place in time.
Interpretation: Patience and reserve will ensure good fortune when the time is right.

Six in the fifth place: When the Emperor's daughter was married, her gown was less ornate than that of her attendant. The moon is almost full; there will be good fortune.

Interpretation: Personal restraint and a lack of ostentation will lead to good fortune in the near future.

Six in the sixth place: The young woman bears an empty basket; the man slaughters a sheep and blood does not flow. There will be no advantage in any direction.
Interpretation: The omens are inauspicious. No good can come of any action performed now.

Hexagram 55

FÊNG

ABUNDANT PROSPERITY

The trigrams: CHÊN: Thunder, arousing. LI: Fire, clinging.

THE DECISION

Abundant prosperity. Progress and development. When the king has achieved his aims he should not fear the change for the worse which must surely follow. Let him instead be as the sun at noon.

COMMENTARY

Here we have great abundance. The trigram representing movement (Chên) is joined to that representing brilliance (Li).

When the king has reached this stage, he has yet further to go. He must cause his brilliance to illuminate all under Heaven. When the sun has reached its zenith, it begins to decline. When the moon has become full, it begins to wane.

The interflow of Heaven and earth is at first vigorous and abundant, then sluggish and scanty, expanding and contracting according to the seasons. How much more is this so with men and with the gods!

Abundant prosperity often gives way to opposing conditions in the affairs of mankind. The ruler who is both forceful and intelligent is able to maintain the prosperity of his realm, and does not fall prey to anxiety. He does not fail in preserving both his position and his abundance. He is like the midday sun, shedding his warmth and light all around.

THE IMAGE

Thunder (Chên) and lightning (Li) together. The superior man arbitrates when disputes arise, and chooses appropriate punishments.

THE LINES

Nine in the first place: He meets a king whose rank equals his own. Although they are similar in character, there will be no clash of personalities. A united advance will win approval.
Interpretation: Co-operation between those who are prosperous serves to consolidate their prosperity.

Six in the second place: He is surrounded by screens so large that they shadow the sky until he can see the stars even at midday. If he tries to enlighten his superior he will only bring down suspicion and distrust upon himself. If he perseveres under these adverse circumstances, applying himself with sincere devotion to his work, there may yet be good fortune.
Interpretation: Although the future looks dark, conditions are nevertheless improving. But he should not try to seek help at this time.

Nine in the third place: A large banner in front of him obscures his vision, but through it he catches a glimpse of a small star at midday. Unable to see ahead clearly, he breaks his right arm; but error will be avoided.
Interpretation: Prevailing conditions will lead to unavoidable misfortune, but glimpses of more hopeful times ahead will tave him from mistakes caused by desperation.

Nine in the fourth place: He finds himself behind a curtain made of material so thick that at noon the sun appears through it as a small star. But he meets there his superior, who is in sympathy with him. There will be good fortune.
Interpretation: The future looks dark and is difficult to de-

fine, but he is not alone. Powerful allies will help him to attain his wishes.

Six in the fifth place: He surrounds himself with men of brilliance and great ability. There will be occasion for congratulation and praise. Good fortune!
Interpretation: Co-operation between able men of good will ensures abundant prosperity.

Six in the sixth place: His large house reflects his prosperity, but when he peers from the door all is still and there is nobody about. For three years no one comes near. There will be evil.
Interpretation: His ostentation alienates him from everyone. Abundance which is so misused can only bring misfortune.

Hexagram 56

LÜ

THE TRAVELLING STRANGER

The trigrams: LI: Fire, clinging. KÊN: Mountain, immovable.

THE DECISION

The travelling stranger. There will be progress and success in small things. If the traveller be firm and correct in his behaviour, good fortune will ensue.

COMMENTARY

Here a weak line occupies the central place of the upper trigram, and responds to the strong lines on either side. This suggests success in small things.

Immovability is here added to fiery brilliance, suggesting progress in minor matters and good fortune for the traveller who is firm and persevering.

Great indeed is the importance of actions taken at this time! Travelling strangers ought to cultivate the qualities of humility and integrity; thus they will escape harm and have success in small matters. A man on the move is unable to attain great things.

THE IMAGE

Fire (Li) on the mountain (Kên): The superior man exercises his cautious wisdom when ordering punishments, and does not allow lawsuits to drag on.

Six in the first place: The traveller is small-minded and involved in trivial affairs. He will bring down calamity upon
himself.

*He has found a sheltered place to rest, and has with him his valuables
and an axe for protection. But he cannot relax and find peace of
mind*

Interpretation: Meddling in minor affairs which are not relevant to one's true business will end in great misfortune.

Six in the second place: The stranger is safe inside his lodgings, together with his valuables. He has good and trustworthy
servants.
Interpretation: Though in a vulnerable position, he retains
his assets and his faithful companions.

Nine in the third place: Through his carelessness his lodgings are burnt down and he loses his servants. However correctly he tries to act, peril is unavoidable.

Interpretation: Through his own actions he jeopardizes his position and loses the loyalty of his former supporters. No matter how hard he tries to make amends the damage has been done and he cannot avoid the danger he has placed himself in.

Nine in the fourth place: He has found a sheltered place to rest, and has with him his valuables and an axe for protection. But he cannot relax and find peace of mind.

Interpretation: Although his position is temporarily secure, it cannot last.

Six in the fifth place: He shoots a pheasant, but loses his arrow in the process. In the end he will receive approval and be given responsibility.

Interpretation: A small setback will soon give place to a major advance.

Nine in the sixth place: A bird burns its own nest. First he laughs, then he cries out. He loses his cow-like docility too easily. There will be evil.

Interpretation: He rejoices at another's misfortune, then finds that he himself is involved in the disaster. Such a loss of equanimity leads to his downfall.

Hexagram 57

GENTLE PENETRATION

The trigrams: SUN: Wind, gentle. SUN: Wind, gentle.

THE DECISION

Gentle penetration. Attainment and progress in small matters. Movement in any direction will be advantageous; so also a meeting with a great man.

COMMENTARY

This hexagram reveals how the commands of the government should be carried out. A strong line occupies the centre of the upper trigram, and its will is carried out effectively. Both the weak lines here are obedient to the strong lines placed above them. Hence it is said that there will be progress in small things, advantage in movement of any kind, and good fortune in meeting with the great man.

The effect of gentle penetration is not to revolutionize or renew, but only to correct and improve. Such delicate correction needs to be directed by a great man if it is to be effective.

THE IMAGE

Winds (Sun) following one another. The superior man impresses his commands on those beneath him, and thus carries through his affairs.

Squatting beneath a couch, he calls on diviners and exorcists in a confused manner

Six in the first place: First he advances, then he retreats. If he had the firm discipline of a soldier it would be to his advantage.
Interpretation: Lacking in vigour and decisiveness, he vacillates.

Nine in the second place: Squatting beneath a couch, he calls on diviners and exorcists in a confused manner. There will be good fortune, and no error.
Interpretation: Although weak and unduly submissive, his efforts are along the right lines and will be fortunate in their outcome.

Nine in the third place: Only by violent and repeated efforts is he able to penetrate. He will have occasion to regret his actions.
Interpretation: All his striving will be ineffective.

Six in the fourth place: While hunting he takes three kinds of game. All occasion for repentance will pass away.
Interpretation: Triumph over adversity assured.

Nine in the fifth place: Perseverance will bring good fortune. Regret will disappear and all his actions will be advantageous. There may not have been a good beginning, but there will be a good end. Let him consider for three days before making any change, and for three further days after the change has been made. Such a course will bring good fortune.
Interpretation: A policy of gentle penetration will result in a fortunate outcome to his present difficulties.

Nine in the sixth place: He crouches beneath a couch, having lost the power to carry out his decisions. However firmly he might act, there will be misfortune.
Interpretation: Gentle penetration carried to excess will lead to loss of authority. Once lost, it cannot easily be retrieved.

Hexagram 58

JOY

The trigrams: TUI: Lake, joyful. TUI: Lake, joyful.

THE DECISION

Joy. There will be progress and success. It will be advantageous to be firm and persevering.

COMMENTARY

This hexagram denotes joyful satisfaction. The centre of each trigram is occupied by a strong line, and the top of each trigram by a weak line: this suggests that the exercise of firm correctness will bring pleasurable advantage.

When the prospect of such pleasure lies before people it beckons them and they forget the heaviness of their labours; when it inspires them to surmount difficulties they forget the danger of death. How great is its power, that it can stimulate people in such a manner!

When the qualities of mildness and harmony prevail without true integrity to control and discipline them, they degenerate. An underlying strength is required if joy is to produce good fortune.

THE IMAGE

Two lakes (Tui) together. The superior man joins in the conversation of friends and their stimulating activities.

Nine in the first place: The pleasure of inward harmony. There will be good fortune.
Interpretation: He is self-sufficient and attracts good fortune to himself.

Nine in the second place: Pleasure arises from inner sincerity. There will be good fortune and all occasion for regret will disappear.
Interpretation: His integrity will ensure that difficulties fall away from him.

Six in the third place: He deliberately surrounds himself with pleasurable things. There will be evil.
Interpretation: Being concerned with external pleasures, he loses his inward peace of mind.

Nine in the fourth place: He hesitates between a choice of pleasures, and cannot rest. He verges on making a wrong decision, then he turns away. The outcome will be joyful.
Interpretation: Careful deliberation and self-examination will resolve his doubts.

Nine in the fifth place: He trusts in one who would injure him. His position is perilous.
Interpretation: Reliance on others rather than on himself leaves him open to betrayal.

Six in the sixth place: He takes pleasure in leading others and attracting them to him.
Interpretation: Experiencing joy in one's power over others is a pleasure only for small men.

Hexagram 59

HUAN

DISPERSION

The trigrams: SUN: Wind, gentle. K'AN: Water, dangerous.

THE DECISION

Dispersion. There will be progress and success. The king
visits his ancestral temple. It will be advantageous to cross the
great water, and to act with firm persistence.

COMMENTARY

There will be progress and success because the centre of
the lower trigram is occupied by a strong line in a position of
power, and also because the weak line at the bottom of the
upper trigram responds to the strong line above it. Because
of this the king approaches his ancestral temple single-mindedly.

He may safely cross the great water because he travels over
the water (K'an) in a vessel made of wood (Sun).

Dispersion results when men's minds are divorced from
what is right and good. Such a process can escalate until it
envelops a kingdom. If sincere piety rules the hearts of men
this will not happen; great undertakings carried out in a disciplined manner will then succeed. But whatever is done, it
must be carried out with careful attention to what is right.

THE IMAGE

Wind (Sun) blowing across the water (K'an). The ancient
kings presented offerings to the Lord of Heaven, and established temples.

Six in the first place: He rescues others from the impending evil, with the help of a strong horse. There will be good fortune.

Interpretation: With the aid of those beneath him he is able to avert the danger.

Nine in the second place: Amidst the growing dispersal he hurries to take shelter behind his altar. Cause for repentance will disappear.

Interpretation: Falling back on his inner spiritual resources in time of crisis will help him to retain his equilibrium.

Six in the third place: He disregards all thought of himself. No cause for regret.

Interpretation: The rejection of all thoughts of self-interest will prevent him getting involved in the general disintegration.

Six in the fourth place: He disperses those who have gathered round him, and picks out a new circle of helpers. Ordinary men would not think that out of dispersal could come a finer re-constitution.

Interpretation: Great clarity of mind is required to pick out the essentials in such a confused situation. This quality is lacking in small men.

Nine in the fifth place: He issues great announcements. Perspiration flows from his body as if it too were taking part in the general dispersion. He distributes the contents of the royal granaries. There will be no error.

Interpretation: Countering a negative kind of dispersal in a daring way by means of positive dispersal (in this case of grain) is justified and laudable.

Nine in the sixth place: He avoids bloodshed and separates himself from the source of his fears. There will be no error.

Interpretation: There is nothing reprehensible in dispersing sources of possible harm.

Hexagram 60

CHIEH

REGULATION

The trigrams: K'AN: Water, dangerous. TUI: Lake, joyful.

THE DECISION

Regulation. There will be progress and success. But if the regulation is too severe and difficult, its good effect will not last long.

COMMENTARY

Progress and attachment are indicated here because the strong and weak lines are equally divided, and the strong lines occupy the central places.

If regulation is too severe, its action will be forced to a standstill. The successful following of a course through perilous conditions gives rise to feelings of pleasure and satisfaction. When regulations are properly controlled by authority, one is able to act freely within a stable framework.

Heaven and earth regulate their functions, and the four seasons complete their cycle accordingly. If rulers formulate their regulations according to such an example, the resources of the state are not depleted and the people suffer no injury.

Regulation is shown in the joints of the bamboo and in the joints of the human body. The seasons of the year are similarly regulated, and on earth regulations are set up by the government for the necessary control and guidance of the people. But if they are to be successful, regulations must be adapted to prevailing conditions, and not always be strict and severe.

THE IMAGE

Water (K'an) across the lake (Tui). The superior man evolves methods of numbering and measurement, and debates points of virtue and right conduct.

THE LINES

Nine in the first place: He does not leave the courtyard outside his door. He makes no error.

Interpretation: Self-restraint at this time is advisable.

Nine in the second place: He does not leave the outer courtyard of his house. There will be evil.

Interpretation: Unnecessary restraint when opportunity presents itself can never result in good fortune.

Six in the third place: He ignores the proper regulations, then later laments. But he has no one to blame but himself.

Interpretation: Regulations must be observed at the proper time if they are to be effective.

Six in the fourth place: Quietly and naturally he observes all regulations. There will be progress and success.

Interpretation: Respect for properly constituted authority will lead to success.

Nine in the fifth place: He submits voluntarily to the regulations he himself has formulated. There will be good fortune, and the outcome of his measures will win him admiration.

Interpretation: The authority given to his regulations by his own public submission to them will ensure their acceptance.

Six in the sixth place: He enforces regulations that are both severe and difficult to maintain. Even when they are obeyed correctly there will still be evil. He will have cause for regret, but this will pass.

Interpretation: Over-severity will bring evil in its wake, but at least it is better than over-indulgence. The evil outcome of harsh regulations can be remedied in time.

Hexagram 61

CHUNG FU

INMOST SINCERITY

The trigrams: SUN: Wind, gentle. TUI: Lake, joyful.

THE DECISION

Inmost sincerity. Good fortune. Even pigs and fishes are moved by it. There will be advantage in crossing the great water, and in being firm and correct.

COMMENTARY

The middle of this hexagram is occupied by two weak lines, and strong lines occupy the centres of the trigrams. Here we have joy combined with gentleness, signifying inmost sincerity. Such sincerity will transform a country!

Sincerity reaches and influences even pigs and fishes. There will be an advantage in crossing the great water, because the symbolism suggests one moving over the lake (Tui) in a boat made of wood (Sun).

In the virtuous exercise of firm correctness we see the proper response of man to the influence of Heaven.

Inmost sincerity is the highest quality open to man, giving him power over spiritual beings, other men, and lower creatures. To attain this state the heart must be free of all consciousness of self. Such selflessness leads to immovable virtue which is flawless and has no vestige of unreality. The man thus gifted will succeed in the most difficult enterprises. Yet even he needs to act firmly in a correct manner.

218

THE IMAGE

Wind (Sun) blowing over the lake (Tui). The superior man gives careful thought to criminal cases and hesitates before invoking the death penalty.

THE LINES

Nine in the first place: He rests inside himself; there will be good fortune. If he sought to rest outside himself he would not succeed.
Interpretation: Reliance on one's inner core of virtue will lead to good fortune.

Nine in the second place: The crane gives voice in her hidden nest, and her young ones respond. It is as if one said, 'I have a bowl of good wine and I will share it with you.'
Interpretation: Such unaffected sincerity evokes a warm response.

Six in the third place: He meets another. He beats a drum intermittently, and weeps and sings alternately.
Interpretation: He looks outside himself rather than within for reassurance, and cannot achieve a state of calm tranquillity.

Six in the fourth place: On a night when the moon is almost full, one of a pair of horses disappears, leaving the other to pull the carriage alone. There will be no error.
Interpretation: Even if he is let down by those he depends on, just as a great moment is approaching, his inmost sincerity is such that he can carry out his plans successfully without them.

Nine in the fifth place: He is perfectly sincere, and links others to him in closest union. There will be no error.
Interpretation: His shining sincerity binds everyone to him.

Nine in the sixth place: He is like a cock trying to reach heaven with his crowing. Even if he acts firmly and correctly there will be evil.

Interpretation: His current good fortune will cause him to over-reach himself; if he had cultivated true sincerity, this would not happen.

Hexagram 62

SMALL SUCCESSES

The trigrams: CHÊN: Thunder, arousing. KÊN: Mountain, immovable.

THE DECISION

Small successes. There will be progress and success, but it will be advantageous to be firm and persevering. Success in small matters but not in great affairs. It is better for the small bird to fly low, where its song can be heard, than to fly too high. In this fashion there will be great good fortune.

COMMENTARY

Here the weak lines exceed the strong lines, denoting their progress and success. But such progress must only take place at the proper time.

The centre of each trigram is occupied by a weak line, therefore the small will succeed and have good fortune. Neither of the strong lines is in a good position of strength, therefore the successes shown will be small and not great.

The passage concerning the small bird indicates that it would be improper to ascend at this time; to descend would be more in keeping with the times.

One must learn to distinguish between what is essential and what is inessential. It is never good to deviate from what is generally recognized as the correct way, where matters of truth are concerned; but in matters of convention or

221

ceremonial such deviation is on occasion permissible. The outward form may be omitted, but the inner truth must be retained.

Even a minor deviation must be undertaken with care, in an attitude of great humility and reverence, and even then only in small matters. Such humility is displayed in the case of the small bird which takes care not to fly too high.

THE IMAGE

Thunder (Chên) over the mountain (Kên). The superior man is exceedingly humble in his conduct, exceedingly sorrowful in mourning, and exceedingly thrifty in his expenditure.

THE LINES

Six in the first place: The bird flies upwards. There will be evil.
Interpretation: Over-confidence leads to unavoidable misfortune.

Six in the second place: He passes by his ancestors and meets his mother. He is unable to reach the ruler, but encounters one of his ministers. There will be no error.
Interpretation: He cannot attain the degree of success he hopes for, but a small success is nothing to be ashamed of.

Nine in the third place: He takes no precautions against danger, and in consequence an inferior finds opportunity to injure him. There will be evil.
Interpretation: Over-confidence in the strength of his own position leaves him open to injury from one he despises.

Nine in the fourth place: He avoids error by countering adversity with restrained action. Any advance will entail danger, and caution is advised. It is unwise to use forceful methods on all occasions.

Interpretation: Knowing when to act and when to refrain from action is the key to small successes in times of adversity.

Six in the fifth place: Dense clouds approach from the western borders, but no rain falls. The prince shoots an arrow and hits a bird in a cave.
Interpretation: Impetuous action at an inappropriate moment disappointment. Lesser expectations will be rewarded.

Six in the sixth place: Unable to exercise self-restraint, he over-reaches himself, like a bird which flies too high in the heavens. There will be evil. The calamity will be self-induced.
Interpretation: Great ambition applied at the wrong time will end in disaster.

Hexagram 63

CHI CHI

COMPLETION ACHIEVED

The trigrams: K'AN: Water, dangerous. LI: Fire, clinging.

THE DECISION

Completion achieved. Progress and success in small matters. There will be advantage in being firm and correct. Good fortune in the beginning will be followed by disorder in the end.

COMMENTARY

There will be advantage in being firm and correct, because the strong and weak lines are properly arranged, each placed correctly.

The position of a weak line in the centre of the lower trigram suggests good fortune, but in the end conditions of order will be exhausted.

The realm is finally at peace, the great water has been safely crossed. Injustices have been rectified and rebellions suppressed. But small things still remain to be done. What has been achieved must be consolidated; the ruler must proceed quietly in the perfection of what has been begun, acting in a firm and correct manner and remaining always aware of the potential instability of human affairs.

THE IMAGE

Water (K'an) over fire (Li). The superior man considers the possibility of future evil, and takes precautionary measures against it.

THE LINES

Nine in the first place: He applies the brake to the wheel of his chariot. He is in the position of the fox who inadvertently wets his tail while crossing a stream. There will be no error.
Interpretation: The time for making swift progress is now past. He should take heed of the omens and desist. A certain loss of face is likely, but this is of small account.

Six in the second place: She loses the screen from her carriage window. She need not search for it; within several days it will be returned to her.
Interpretation: Vigorous action is not appropriate at this time. Restraint will allow circumstances to set themselves right in due season.

Nine in the third place: The Illustrious Ancestor, Emperor Wu Ting, made war on the land of the demons, but took three years to subdue it. Small men should not be employed in large enterprises.
Interpretation: The completion of a major enterprise is not out of the question, but it would take so long as to leave one in a state of exhaustion.

Six in the fourth place: He collects rags all day to stop any leak in his boat, and stays on his guard all day.
Interpretation: He exercises prudence and a watchful caution against impending evil.

Nine in the fifth place: The neighbour in the east slaughters an ox for his sacrifice; but the small spring sacrifice of the neighbour in the west receives the blessing.

Interpretation: A small offering made with sincerity at the right time is of more worth than a large one made at an inappropriate moment.

Six in the sixth place: Even his head is immersed! His position is perilous.
Interpretation: Impetuous action at an inappropriate moment will involve him in great danger.

Hexagram 64

WEI CHI

BEFORE COMPLETION

The trigrams: LI: Fire, clinging. K'AN: Water, dangerous.

THE DECISION

Before completion. Progress and success. The fox has almost crossed the stream when it gets its tail wet. There will be no advantage in any way.

COMMENTARY

Progress and success is indicated here because the central position of the upper trigram is occupied by a weak line.

The fox is said to have nearly crossed the stream, revealing that he has not yet completely escaped from danger.

The fox wets his tail and can win no advantage because the success shown at the beginning is not carried through to the end. Although the lines are not in places appropriate to them, yet strong lines and weak lines respond to each other.

Just as the seasons of the year constantly change and pursue their recurring cycle, so it is with the phases of society. Order is finally achieved, and then it passes. Thereupon the struggle recommences for its realization once more. The fox symbolizes him who at such times tries to correct the general disorder. His efforts cannot be successful, and he can only involve himself in trouble and danger. That which can be achieved must be undertaken in other ways.

THE IMAGE

Fire (Li) over the water (K'an). The superior man carefully discriminates between things before arranging them in the positions they should naturally occupy.

THE LINES

Six in the first place: The fox wets its tail. There will be misfortune.
Interpretation: A serious misjudgement will involve him in error and even disgrace.

Nine in the second place: He applies the brake to the wheel of his carriage. Firm correctness will bring about good fortune.
Interpretation: Powerful restraint will have a happy outcome.

Six in the third place: He tries to advance further, leaving important matters unfinished. This will lead to evil. But there will still be advantage in trying to cross the great water.
Interpretation: Restraint is called for at the present time, but one should keep one's aim in mind.

Nine in the fourth place: By acting firmly and correctly he attains good fortune, and loses all occasion for regret. Let him gather his forces, as if he were about to invade the land of the demons! After a three-year struggle he and his companions will be richly rewarded.
Interpretation: Entering into a major enterprise at this time will entail a long and exhausting struggle, but if he resolves to continue to the end the outcome will be highly successful.

Six in the fifth place: By the exercise of firm correctness he obtains good fortune, and has no occasion for regret. He possesses inward sincerity and displays the brightness of the superior man. There will be good fortune.

Interpretation: The omen is one of complete success and achievement.

Nine in the sixth place: Full of confidence, he feasts quietly with his friends. There will be no error. But if he cultivates his confidence to excess, like a fox who allows his head to be immersed while crossing the stream, then his downfall is assured.

Interpretation: One has the right to enjoy the fulfilment of one's ambitions, but even here self-restraint is still required if continuing success is to be maintained.

APPENDIX 1

Mathematical Aspects of the I Ching

The ancient Chinese saw the universe as being closed and finite, cyclical rather than linear. Numbers were symbols used to classify time and space.

The number 1 was not the first in a series continuing to infinity, but was the symbol of the heart of the universe. Simple numbers, such as 2, 3, 4, and 5, being close to the centre, were emblems of the primary and most powerful processes of change.

Numbers were the messengers of Heaven, making clear the relationships between apparently disparate phenomena, and indicating the changes which might be expected to follow from them.

Therefore the connection in China between mathematics and divination was always particularly close. The word for calculation, *suan,* is closely related to a word meaning divine revelation. This can lead to confusion when early texts are being translated, as it is often not easy to tell whether the writer is discussing arithmetic or prognostication.

The symbolical application of numbers was from the earliest times accepted as the best method of achieving a state of rapport with the basic cycles of nature. The universe was first divided into the opposing but complementary principles of Heaven and Earth (later referred to as Yang and Yin).

Heaven was indicated by the number 1, and Earth by the number 2. But because the number 1 was considered to be too abstract, too ideal to be involved in the processes of change, it was instead assigned to represent the totality of existence, while Heaven as an active principle was instead indicated by the number 3. This was considered highly satisfactory, because Heaven (3) was then seen to embrace Earth (2).

Following this line of reasoning, all even numbers were assigned to Earth and all odd numbers to Heaven.

According to the Commentary on the Appended Judgements (*Hsi Tz'u Chuan*): *To Heaven belongs the number 1, to Earth 2; to Heaven 3, to Earth 4; to Heaven 5, to Earth 6; to Heaven 7, to Earth; to Heaven 9, to Earth 10.*

The numbers belonging to Heaven are five, and those belonging to Earth are five. The two series of numbers correspond to one another, and each number has its mate. The Heavenly numbers add up to 25, and the Earthly numbers to 30. The total of the numbers of Heaven and Earth together is 55. It is through these that the changes and transformations are completed, and the gods and spirits kept in movement.

The commentry then goes on briefly to describe the divinatory process, explaining the symbolic significance of the numbers that occur:

The total number (of yarrow stalks) is 50, of which 49 are used. They are divided into two heaps to represent the two (Heaven and Earth). One is then taken (from the right-hand heap) to symbolize the three powers (Heaven, Earth, and man.) They (the two heaps) are then counted off by fours to represent the four seasons, and those that remain are put aside to represent the intercalary month. Because there are two intercalary months every five years, there are two such operations. Afterwards the whole is repeated.

This is particularly interesting in that it does show the kind of thinking which linked the abstract world of numbers with the concrete world of natural phenomena.

The Chinese at this time used a lunar calendar that required the addition of two extra months in every five years to bring it into line with the solar year. Perhaps the choice of fifty yarrow stalks is derived from the five-yearly cycle, though this is by no means certain. The student who attempts to explore this particular field soon finds himself shifting ground, as the significance of particular numbers to the ancient Chinese is far from clear.

2 and 3 are primary numbers of Earth and Heaven, but 4 and 5 indicate their 'proper places', from which they give rise

231

to the processes of change. The next four numbers, 6, 7, 8, and 9, are those which actually represent major points in the cycles of phenomena. These four are the 'Ritual Numbers' that occur in I Ching consultations.

7 indicates the movement of Heaven at an early stage, when it is still 'Young Yang'. As the cycle proceeds it becomes 'Old Yang', represented by 9.

8 indicates Earth near the commencement of the cycle, or 'Young Yin', while 6 represents 'Old Yin', the negative principle in action.

7 advances to 9, and 8 retreats to 6.

When consulting the Oracle by the yarrow stalk method you will find that Young Yang lines and Young Yin lines can both be indicated by three different aggregates of stalks, while Old Yang lines and Old Yin lines can only be indicated by one aggregate each (see the table on page 36).

Your hexagram is therefore less likely to contain moving (Old) lines than non-moving (Young) lines. Thus when a moving line does occur it is of particular significance, and the Duke of Chou's words concerning it must be consulted.

The groups of numbers which are arrived at by process of counting through the stalks four at a time (e.g. 9+8+4, or 5+4+8) are related to the Ritual Numbers in the following way:

At the first counting of the stalks, the first stalk, the one held between the little finger and ring finger, is not included, therefore a total of 9 is counted as 8, and a total of 5 is counted as 4.

The number 4 is seen as a single unit, and is assigned to Heaven, which is symbolized by the number 3.

The number 8 is regarded as a double unit and is assigned to Earth, symbolized by the number 2.

At the second and third counting of the stalks the same process of reduction is gone through, 4 counting as 3 and 8 counting as 2.

If these reduced numbers are then added together, the relevant Ritual Numbers are arrived at. For example:

$$5\,(3)+4\,(3)+8\,(2) = 8 \quad \text{a Young Yin line}$$
$$9\,(2)+8\,(2)+8\,(2) = 6 \quad \text{an Old Yin line}$$

The arithmetic we normally use has the base 10. By adding a zero to any number we multiply it by 10. The mathematician Leibniz (1646–1716) first realized the possibility of an arithmetic to the base 2. The 2-scale of notation, which is called the binary or dyadic scale, multiplies any number by only 2 when a zero is added to it.

For example, the first ten numbers in our familiar scale would appear thus in the binary scale:

1 =	1	6 =	110
2 =	10	7 =	111
3 =	11	8 =	1000
4 =	100	9 =	1001
5 =	101	10 =	1010

Leibniz first described the binary system in a paper entitled *De Progressione Dyadica* published in 1679. Between the years 1697 and 1702 he corresponded with one of the Jesuit missionaries in China, Père Joachim Bouvet, and in 1698 Père Bouvet brought to Leibniz's notice the hexagrams of the I Ching, as offering a curious parallel to his binary system of arithmetic.

Leibniz acquired a copy of the old diagram showing the hexagrams displayed in a circle and a square (pages 24–5). He discovered that if he substituted a zero for each broken line and a 1 for each unbroken line, the hexagrams would illustrate his own binary scale from the numbers zero to 63.

For example, the hexagram Po (second from the left on the top row in the square, and almost at the bottom in the circle) is 1 in the binary scale, if zeros preceding 1 are ignored. Hexagram Pi, to the right of Po, is 2 (expressed 10 in the binary scale), and so on.

If you wish to test this for yourself, the easiest way is to start with a number in our familiar 10-scale, then convert it into the 2-scale. To do this you divide the number by 2, write the quotient on the next line, and write the remainder on the side. Then divide the quotient by 2, put the new quotient on the next line, and the remainder on the side. Continue in this way until you get a quotient equal to zero. The column of remainders at the side is the number you started with expressed in the binary scale.

To convert this into a hexagram, draw a broken line by each zero and an unbroken line by each 1. This will give you the hexagram that corresponds to the number you began with.

Here is an example. Find the hexagram corresponding to the number 50.

$$
\begin{array}{ll}
2) \ 50 & \\
2) \ 25 & 0 \\
2) \ 12 & 1 \\
2) \ \ 6 & 0 \\
2) \ \ 3 & 0 \\
2) \ \ 1 & 1 \\
\ \ \ \ 0 & 1 \\
\end{array}
$$

CHIEH
Hexagram 50 in the traditional diagram

If you find that your result works out in less than the six lines needed to form a hexagram, just add extra zeros to the bottom of the calculation until the requisite six lines are made up. For example:

$$
\begin{array}{ll}
2) \ 9 & \\
2) \ 4 & 1 \\
2) \ 2 & 0 \\
2) \ 1 & 0 \\
\ \ \ 0 & 1 \\
& 0 \\
& 0 \\
\end{array}
$$

KÊN
Hexagram 9

The order of the hexagrams given in the diagram on pages 24–5 does not correspond with that given in the body of the text,

234

and seems to have originated with the Sung philosopher Shao Yung, around A.D. 1060.

Leibniz had rediscovered a mathematical system which had been lost for at least six hundred years. It cannot be proved that the inventors of the hexagrams back in the Chou dynasty realized the mathematical significance of their work, as the order in which the hexagrams are arranged in the oracle gives no indication of the binary system.

The I Ching, however, like the binary system, is based on the permutations of two digits or quantities. Today's electronic computer operates on the same system, having thermionic valves or electronic switches (called flip-flop circuits) which have two positions. One turns the current on and the other turns it off. These two positions are represented by the numbers 1 and 0. 1 for on, and 0 for off.

A linked series of such switches can form a number in the binary scale – or a hexagram!

Finally, it has been discovered that the neurons in the central nervous systems of human beings and other higher animals obey the same rules. They are either 'on' or 'off'. That is, either completely passive or else acting almost without reference to the power or nature of the stimulus which triggered them.

In view of these modern developments, the tradition that the inventors of the I Ching devised the 64 hexagrams to reflect the inner nature of all phenomena appears less unlikely and less futile than it otherwise might.

Perhaps the age of the electronic computer and specialized sciences such as neurology will paradoxically bring about a new appreciation of the ancient Oracle of Change.

The Development of the
I Ching in China

The eight trigrams that form the basis of the Oracle of Change are known to have been in existence at a very early date. Records speak of an oracle book known as the Lien Shan being used during the Hsia dynasty (traditionally 2205–1766 B.C.), while Confucius refers to the oracle of the Shang dynasty (traditionally 1766–1150 B.C.), called Kuei Ts'ang.

The I Ching as we know it today was probably originated by King Wên, precursor of the Chou dynasty, around the year 1143 B.C. Wên's son Tan, the Duke of Chou, added his line-interpretations some forty years later, and the book circulated widely under the title Chou I, or the Change of Chou.

Confucius devoted much time to the study of this work in the years prior to his death in 479 B.C., and probably composed one of the commentaries on it which are traditionally ascribed to him. Other commentaries were added by pupils and later followers of Confucius. It was at this time that the much-enlarged book became elevated to the status of a Confucian Classic, and was entitled the I Ching, or Classic of Change.

The I Ching escaped the great book-burning of 213 B.C., after which time it further consolidated its reputation as an oracle and textbook of magic. Its fame spread even further after 124 B.C., when an imperial university was founded for the express purpose of teaching the Confucian scriptures. The importance of this university can be gauged from the fact that 30,000 students were enrolled there.

In A.D. 175 the texts of the Confucian Classics were engraved on stone, and this was repeated during the period A.D. 240–48. Around this time the influential scholar Wang Pi (A.D. 226–49) emphasized the value of the I Ching as a manual of philosophy.

During the Sung dynasty (A.D. 960–1279) neo-Confucian scholars edited and revised the entire Confucian Canon, including the I Ching. At this time the various commentaries were divided among the hexagrams to which they referred.

This version, with an added commentary by the Sung philosopher Chu Hsi (1130–1200), became the orthdox one until a new edition was prepared during the K'ang Hsi period (1662–1722). The K'ang Hsi edition, first published in 1715, re-separated the commentaries from the main body of the text. To it was added an anthology of quotations from the works of 218 scholars, ranging in time from the second century B.C. down to the seventeenth century A.D.

This last version has formed the basis of most modern European translations of the I Ching. Various minor editions of greater or lesser completeness have appeared in China since 1715, but the imperial K'ang Hsi edition is generally admitted to be scholastically the most reliable.

APPENDIX 3

European Translations of the I Ching

REGIS, P., *Y-King, antiquissimus Sinarum liber*. Paris, 1834.

The first translation, by Jesuit missionaries, of the I Ching into a Western language.

MCCLATCHIE, Rev. Canon, *A translation of the Confucian Yî King, or the 'Classic of Changes'*, with notes and appendix. Shanghai, 1876

A weird attempt 'to open the mysteries of the Yî by applying to it the key of Comparative Mythology'.

DE HARLEZ, C., *Le Yih-King, Texte Primitif Rétabli, Traduit et Commenté*. Bruxelles, 1889

An interesting early translation, but unreliable by modern standards.

LEGGE, J., *The Texts of Confucianism, Pt II, the Yi King*. Oxford, 1899

A careful and literal translation from the K'ang Hsi edition of 1715. Legge, however, did not believe in the I Ching's powers as an oracle, and his comments tend to be derisory. The method of divination is not clearly explained.

WILHELM, R., *I Ging; das Buch der Wandlungen*. Jena, 1924 (2 vols.)

English translation by C. F. Baynes under the title *The I Ching or Book of Changes*. New York and London 1950 (2 vols)

The fullest and most sympathetic translation yet made, with excellent introductory material and a profound foreword by Dr C. G. Jung. The book is unfortunately marred by confusing layout and typography.

BLOFELD, J., *The Book of Change*. London, 1965

An interesting recent translation by an English scholar now resident in Bangkok. Outlines the divinatory aspect of the I Ching very fully. The Confucian commentaries are omitted.

SIU, R. G. H. *The Man of Many Qualities; A legacy of the I Ching*. Cambridge, Mass., 1968

A new translation of the words of King Wên and the Duke of Chou, together with over 700 excerpts from world literature which serve to illustrate them. An original and fascinating approach to the oracle.

APPENDIX 4

How to obtain a set of sticks suitable for I Ching consultations:
An authentic set of yarrow stalks for use when consulting the oracle would have to be gathered from where the plant grows wild in the countryside. Ideally, everyone should dry the stalks, and prepare their own. But sticks made from split bamboo can be bought and these form an adequate substitute. They can probably be supplied from the following booksellers:

The Atlantis Bookshop Ltd
49a Museum Street
London W.C.1.

John M. Watkins, Ltd
19–21 Cecil Court
London W.C.2.